A Wildness of the Heart

A Wildness of the Heart

Limerent Object and other stories

Madison Scott-Clary

Also by Madison Scott-Clary

Qoheleth + Gallery Exhibition

ally

Eigengrau

Restless Town

Arcana — A Tarot Anthology, ed.

Rum and Coke — Three Short Stories from a Furry Convention

All characters are fictional and any resemblance to actual people, living or dead, is unintentional. The town of Sawtooth, ID is, with apologies to the residents of the real town Sawtooth City, fictional as well, and not intended to represent any one particular place.

This book uses the fonts Gentium Book Basic, DejaVu Sans, and Tom's New Roman and was typeset with X_ƎL^AT_EX.

ISBN: 978-1-948743-21-1

A Wildness of the Heart

Cover © 2021 Nomax
www.patreon.com/nomax

First Edition, 2021.

Jump

Some folks, they're just built to jump.

Sim, you know, he was quick to jump at any opportunity, 'cause when Sim sees an opening, there was just no other possible steps for him to take. That's how Sim works. Sim jumps, can't help but.

So Sim jumped when there was that convenience store. He jumped 'cause the gun was under the seat in their shitty beater van and the convenience store had a completely empty parking lot and the lights were on and he couldn't see the clerk.

Isolated, too. You know the type. One of those buildings that sits squat by the side of the road and probably a ton of truckers come through there and the clerks are busy from something like seven to eleven, but it's not big enough to actually be a 7-Eleven. But then the truckers' clocks run out and they all go pull over at one of the big TransAmericas down the road where they've got the hot showers and the hot meals and the reasonably attractive waitresses in that homey, no-nonsense way, who smirk but never flirt back.

See, one of those places, after the day truckers' clocks run out and before the night truckers come by, there's these few hours where everything's quiet and the clerk is just sitting behind that counter, behind that plexiglass or whatever they put up there, and he could call the cops or state patrol, sure, but he's far enough away from everything that he was basically told in training a week or two back to let robbers take everything and trust the cameras to get the plate details and only then call.

Sim saw the opportunity, Sim jumped, just how he's built.

And where Sim jumped, there was Ursula. Sim was the brains, he'd say. He'd run the plan by Ursula three times whether or not she got it on the first time through. And she was the muscle, big old bear like her, nothing getting past if she needed to block the door, and if she need to knock heads, Sim said, she would just have to knock some heads.

But see, this convenience store, something had clearly happened there. Clerk'd been holding it for until all those truckers' clocks ran out because he was too busy and the owner was too cheap to hire anyone else, so he had to steal a moment of quiet at eleven thirty or whatever, and he ran off to the bathroom out around the back of the building. Sometimes you just gotta go, you know?

Sometimes you forget, too. Ever forget? Happens to me, forget little things all the time. Poor clerk, he was good at remembering, only this time he forgot to lock the front door and forgot to close out the drawer.

And this just happened to be the time when a ferret and a bear came tearing down the highway and slipped right up to the front of the store all nice like, quiet, no uncouth squealing of tires under those bright lot lights and the moon beyond. They hop out like maybe they got just a quick errand to run, and clerk, he hears them and figures he's got enough time to finish up, but they're in and out real smooth.

"Shit, Ursula," we can imagine Sim saying with that reedy tenor that can cut through anything like it was paper. "How fuckin' perfect is this? All laid out for us."

A mumble.

"Grab a snack, girlie, I don't care. Hell, grab all the snacks, anything you need. You need pills? Grab some pills. Condoms? Hah!"

A mumble.

"Christ, of course grab the drawer first." A pause, then a high laugh. "Fine, ya big dummy. I'll get the drawer, you grab our snacks or pills or whatever. Oh, shit, yeah, grab me like a whole box of Snickers or whatever. I'll mow through those."

And poor clerk hears his drawer being yanked free and here he is, his drawers down around his ankles and he cusses and cusses and cusses and maybe starts crying, but at this point it's just too late, so he keeps sitting his skinny ass down on the toilet until he hears the rev of an engine, the thrum and rattle of something with a couple hundred thousand miles on it, maybe got fifty more in it, and then he hears it fade into the dark, and only then does he call.

"Do you *see* this? Hah! Did you get a load of that take?" says that ferret as the unassuming minivan trundles down the road, no more'n five over the limit. "Shit, poor fella in there probably didn't even have time to hit the safe after his shift, and where was he anyway?"

Ursula, she keeps her eyes on the road, troops past the fields, past the cars, past the troopers parked on the sides of the highway. Turns once, turns again, on through Sawtooth and then they're up in the Rockies, poking along through the scrub and the sand and the high desert. Nothing out here, 'course, not even a tent or trailer. Just a place to park that big old van of theirs out where no one bothers looking.

And Sim, he's already jumping from the passenger seat. He's already dancing and twirling around the front of the van, those parking lights catching him only from the waist down — always such a dancer, that ferret — but you can surely imagine him pirouetting along between sagebrush and scrub pine with that raggedy-ass tail of his flip-flopping behind him, laughing away.

"Ursula, Ursula! Come on girlie, come on you big dummy," he calls. "Come on out. Gosh! Gosh, I love you darling! I love you so much I feel like my whole heart's gonna burst and you'd have to patch me back up again. Look at this! I didn't want to freak you out on the road, I know you get all skittish behind the wheel, 'specially after a job, but gosh I love you. Just full of love from tip to tail. There's like six thousand dollars in that take. Six thousand dollars *and* a box of Snickers! What else you grab? Snacks? Get your pills? Hah!"

And the bear is out the van now and parking her backside against the front of the grill and Sim dances around her, taking first one paw and then t'other, lifting her arms up so that he can twirl about beneath them, smacking her belly, hitting her thighs with his tail, kicking up dust into the midnight air.

"We got it made, now." He finally flops all along the front of Ursula, stretched up long as he can so he can get his skinny arms around the mountain of her shoulders, and sure, she can smell the candy bar on his breath. "We can go straight now, you know? Hit up another small town, Mountain Home or Newsom or something, park our asses, get out of the risky business.

"But listen, my darling, my dear. Hey, hey, listen. You gotta try'n understand my plan. There's so much to it we gotta do first. Six 'kay or whatever will buy us a few months, but you know you and you know me. We gotta still earn something so long as we're not totally on our own, you know? Gotta earn our keep best we can so we can eat and gas and keep up the van.

"I know you been wanting to go straight for years now, get out of the job-to-job life and go do something that's day-to-day, and I love you, you big oaf, you big dummy, but maybe we hit up just one or two more once we get there, real sly-like without raising any eyebrows, or maybe we do it on the way, just to be sure, and I promise no more cards or dice.

"Ursula, my dear, my love, you okay keepin' those muscles up for me a few more days? Just a few more. Just a few more runs, just a few more heads to knock together, you understand. I swear on my life, girlie, I swear up and down your body from those ears you know I love to bite to that hot fuckin' cunt–" this punctuated with a grab at her groin, 'cause Sim'll always jump to that, he's just built to. "–to those big fuckin' feet of yours, you'll get to live the straight life soon. We been on the road so many years now — what, like twenty or something? — and sooner or later you'll bury those feet of yours in some good clean earth instead of in some poor sop's stomach and that earth will be your very own garden. You'll have it all for yourself!"

And Sim is off spinning again, spinning into the dark, and surely Ursula's got a smile or something going on as he calls out to her — "Two gardens! A row of carrots in front cause I know you love those and maybe a whole fuckin' mess of beets out back" — but we'll never know, will we? Sim won't settle his eyes on her long enough, he's too busy jumping.

And let's just suppose they managed it. Let's just picture what that looks like, Ursula dressed in those coveralls that fit her just so, standing up to her ankles in good clean earth, turned over and over with peat and that sheep shit fertilizer that somehow manages to smell like it could grow things even on the moon. We can just imagine, if we like, that Ursula'd plow furrows herself with those handfuls of claws, dropping seeds in their wake. We can suppose that she'd baby those beets until she could cradle them herself, plucked fresh from the earth. Would she kiss them, you think? Would she sing them lullabies? Surely fresh-grown beets make a hell of a stew.

But still, they had got to earn their keep, hadn't they? That's what Sim said, kept saying, would always say at the drop of a hat, at the drop of a haul, every time they hopped in the van after a heist or holdup. He'd promise her late at night in bed, and maybe he'd even call out to her across a gas station or over the hood of some poor sop's car as the fox or cat or whatever shrieked and threw coins at her feet and recoiled in terror.

So with the courage of the sun or the moon or a kite jerking tight at its tether, Ursula might could just keep at her routine, we imagine, still doing her runs in the morning and hauling big old rocks round here and there just to keep those shoulders from getting too soft and brushing her fur out in the evenings. Still crunching on those carrots we all know she loves and buying cans of beets — pale imitations of those in her dreams — to go with cheap chuck so she can cook up a stew on the tailgate of the van, just past the end of their mattress. Still letting Sim push her down onto that very same mattress after every job, cause we all know the ferret's gotta jump every opportunity he gets and the jobs, they make him jumpy, and maybe she makes a sound or maybe not, 'cause we already know how taciturn our Ursula is, quiet to her core, and we'll never know her thoughts as he hunches and curls above her because Sim hasn't the time to listen after making, he promises himself, love to her, he's too busy rolling right into sleep.

All supposition, 'course. All we know, all we know and of course all poor Sim knows, is that our Ursula's heart beats faster.

We all heard a fair bit of this before in the papers and the gossip and the chatter, 'cause they caught old Sim, poor fella, caught him in the end. Caught him and he was yelling and wailing and jumping about, rambling to the cops and anyone who'd listen, but the rest only we really, truly know.

Because they never caught our Ursula, never caught the bear and her dreams and her brawn and all her unspoken words and all her unsmiled smiles. Never caught her, and if they never caught her, did she ever really exist, you suppose? Exist and live and ride along all those heists? Did she ever really let Sim push her back onto that mattress? Did she ever haul rocks or run miles or knock heads or crunch carrots?

We know she did, 'course we do. We really, truly know.

Certainly others did as well. Others must'a seen her, at least as a shadow. Sim and t'other, Sim and the big'un, who'd hit up stores and gas stations and foxes and cats. But did Sim know? Did Sim really know just how very present she was and how often she dreamed of burying her feet in good clean earth, in her own garden? We can surely say he saw her and that he felt her and that he fucked her and that he must be talking to someone, but whether or not he only danced around her and defined her presence or what he imagined it to be by his very unknowing, we can't rightly say.

All we can say was she snapped that very night. We can't know how many times she'd dreamed the dream of gardens and beets and moons and freedom any more than we can know just how many times before that lucky take that Sim promised her they'd go straight, had bit her ear, made promises, and kept on jumping, how many months he'd promised her years of freedom or how many years he'd promised decades, how many times had told her that he, he promised himself, loved her.

We can, like Sim, just like the ferret, only dance around that very unknowing and divine by ping-ponging around a hidden center that she must've, that night after Sim fucked her and fell right asleep, craved her garden and beets and the moon and freedom more than she might have cared to haul rocks or run miles or knock heads, more than she cared even to crunch her carrots. Defining an absence by walking its muddy shores.

And thus in the wee small hours of the morning we know that Sim, too busy jumping, never kept the batteries in the flashlight charged, so it's a damn weak light that bobs and bounces its way up the dirt trail from where they'd made their camp that night, that camp up the hills from Sawtooth, and it's not bobbing from his endless dancing now, 'cause someone down in town told him they'd seen Ursula heading up into the mountains. Someone there said the bear'd been wandering a fair piece away from where they were camped late at night long after they'd gone to sleep.

Not dancing, no. We can guess our poor Sim is troubled by the way he stomps and skitters, first one then t'other with sage brush and scrub pine casting shifting shadows. Stomping and cussing cause he was afraid of the Rockies, up where the air gets clean and bright in the nose and the throat and the trees practically shine and there's certainly no hauls to be had or plans to be made. Afraid, perhaps, though we can be sure one such as he would never say so.

"Big dummy. Trespassin' up these hills, I'm sure, this's gotta be someone's land, just gotta be," he says to that dim circle of light on the ground and to the darkling trees and to the moon up high. "Imagine a big girl like her needing to go for a nature hike, taking those big-ass feet of hers to soak them in streams or bury them in pine needles or — hah! — bearberry. Imagine needing to take a vacation from bein' stronger'n I'll ever be. Imagine needing to take a break from having a life so easy as the one I bought for her. Big dummy, I swear.

"Just you wait-" Though who this 'you' is we'll likely never know. Maybe that very same moon. "Just you wait. She'll be comin' back looking all peaceful and full of the light of the stars or maybe she's up there meditating on a rock like some golden Buddha you see in all those shows I'm sure she likes. Just you wait! She'll come back with a big dumb grin on that big blank face of hers, and I'll jump up and say, 'You been rollin' around in needles again, girlie? You been out there having a romp with the deer? You climbin' trees and howlin' at the moon?' And I'll say, 'You look a fool like that, pine-cones in your ears. You look a total fool thinkin' all your peace is bound up in quiet and not in the life I'm buyin'.'"

But far out, miles away by now, Ursula runs her hardest. She plows through the trees because she will not stop, cannot stop, could not hope to stop. Nowhere to go, nowhere to be, she leaves a wake through the carpet of needles.

She runs until the trees run out and she has to make a wake through shale and scree, through stone and snow, and our Ursula keeps on running. She runs until the mountain runs out and the earth yawns open beneath her feet and all she has to make waves in is stars and the good clean black of the night.

And she lets her arms spread away in a flourish of a bow, a genteel curtsy to no one but the moon, and those arms become stars, they become stars of brightest white because what better color could a star ever hope to be? Stars to wrap around the moon.

And she lets her legs drift loose like a garment long past its prime hung out to dry, like those coveralls that fit just so, the ones she'd been mending years and years now, darning by camp stove and headlight and in plain light of day, suspending that baseness. They fall away and burn into that crisp brightness, standing stark as stars against the fabric of the night. They burn as bright as her arms, for every rock Ursula hauled or head she knocked, surely she'd ran a mile.

And she sheds the mantle of the weight of the world, letting her shoulders drop down as easy as could be, sloughing off cares as easy as the skin of beets boiled just long enough, as easy as Sim dancing in the lights of the van earlier that night, back out in the foothills. Shoulders relaxing as easy as it was to jump.

And thus lets her belly fall away like an apron full of boulders, that ever-soft curve no longer held taut to keep Sim from poking fun at it as he fucked her, hunching and curling above her and pretending like she was with child or fat as could be. Those boulders, too, they become stars in the sky, burning as bright as anything.

And at long last she is able to reach up to the moon with the stars that were her, reach up to the moon that one last time, and give the face held within a kiss, leaving behind a twinkle of her eye, one last star, shining bright as all get-out, to show her love for the night and for the moon and for the good clean earth below.

And now there's nothing left of our Ursula but her yearning, insatiable shadow cast upon the ground as the moon rises ever higher and the stars wheel and dance and Sim cusses his cusses and the lights of the town twinkle below, and all we can do is hope that at last she gets to bury her feet in good clean earth and sow her carrots and beets, and if ever someone hunches and curls above her in labor or in lust or in pain or in joy, all we can do is hope that it will be out of more than a mere promise of love.

Nothing left but a yearning shadow and those stars, 'cause some folks are just plain built to jump, but some were born to shine.

Limerent Object

εκαρδίωσας ημάς ενί από οφθαλμών σου εν μία ενθέματι τραχήλου σου

You have ravished my heart with one glance of your eyes, with one bead of your necklace.

1

I wrap emotions in the cool embrace of jargon to soften sharp edges and take the sting out of ones I feel too keenly. It's why I got into this field. It's why I studied what I did. Of course I care for my clients, and of course I love what I do, but my reason for being here, for being a psychologist, is a simple insatiable need to explain away my emotions.

I've talked about it with my therapist at length[1]. We talk about my need to hide behind words as a way of reducing my vulnerability. They become armor, cover, camouflage when taken in this sense.

There's a tension, then, between these two explanations: to put it the way I did at the beginning is to allow words to be a useful tool to define the edges of my emotions and perhaps make them easier to digest and understand in the process.

To hear Jeremy's suggestion, though, my words are a means by which I might reduce my responsibility to actually feel the emotions I strive to define.

Thus me, sitting here on my lunch break, writing a journal on the steno pad I use in sessions.

Despite the utility I know there to be within the act of journaling, something which I've recommended to countless patients of mine, it's never quite something that I've picked up for myself. I always felt like maybe I was supposed to do something *more* than just write about what I had done during the day, so I'd go off onto long philosophical tangents like this, and then I'd start to feel guilty for not writing about what I'd done during the day. No matter what,

---

[1]We all have them, therapist-therapists. I would never trust a therapist who does not.

it felt like I was doing something wrong, like I was incorrectly doing the thing I knew how to describe to those who looked to me for instruction.

When I'd brought this fact up to Jeremy, he laughed and called me a "fucking nerd"[2] and then talked me through what we thought my goals should be:

- I should write about the feelings that I have during the day until I've finished a complete thought about them, and then stop.
- If an event comes up, I should feel free to record it, but not feel obligated to.

It sounds almost simplistic, but I get what he's doing. He's giving me permission to write about feelings instead of actions, to not feel bad about, as he put it, "leaning on [my] upbringing and the way [I] think in complete sentences and five paragraph essays". Of course, along with that, he wants me to actually feel things and process them rather than just wrap them up with a label and set them on a shelf. Use my strengths to shore up my weaknesses.

So, what am I weak at?

I think I'm weak at processing my emotions in a way that feels like growth. I wrap them up in words and I try to talk my way through processing them, but it's a performative sort of vulnerability that doesn't lead to any growth. As a result, I wind up in one of two situations:

- I feel the same things over and over again with no change in how I process them; or

---

[2]A term I originally used on myself in a fit of self-deprecation which Jeremy occasionally tosses back at me when I am being particularly obstinate.

- I feel new things that I've never felt before, and rather than try to understand them, I shove them off to the side as unexplainable.

The latter is something that I've been making some progress at recently, as I learn to improve my emotional literacy, but the former is a habit that I need to break.

To go along with this task, then, what are my strengths?

I would say that Jeremy pinned them down quite neatly. I think that my upbringing, strict as it was, instilled in me a sense of duty — first to my parents, then to my school, then to God and my time in seminary, and now to my patients. Also, he is not wrong in joking about thinking in essays; being so bound up in language is a net positive in that it allows me to take what clients tell me and turn it into something actionable for them, just as it previously allowed me to take the scripture that I read and turn it around through hermeneutics and truly understand it in a way that simply living as a believer would not.

Alright, so how can I build up the weaker portion of myself with my strengths?

I think that the best way to put the goal is to use my language skills to journal about emotions so that I have a record. If I could study scripture and study psychology, then surely I can study my own notes and from there, learn and grow to handle my emotions in a more deliberate and constructive fashion, right? Basically, write what I feel and how I react so that next time I can react better.

All of this, however many hundreds of words, all because I told Jeremy that I think I have a crush on a girl and didn't know what to do about it.

Ah well, I suppose that this has already been therapeutic, in its own way. I have a task I can set for myself, and, knowing me, all I need to do is let my sense of duty loose on it and we'll see if it bears any fruit in the weeks and months to come.

2

I was struck by a sudden memory today, during my final session of the day.

I was seeing a young wolf who was struggling with getting settled in his degree at university and feeling guilty for not taking to it right off the bat, and I had a sudden recollection about leaving Saint John's, all those years ago. It was strange to feel that sudden demanding of attention come over me, that rush that required me to think about the past *right now*, with no recourse to avoid it. It led to an unintended silence between me and my patient.

"So, I don't know," he said after the silence grew uncomfortable. "What do you think?"

I don't remember quite how I came to the decision to share, but I suppose I must have weighed my options and figured it might be worth it to bring the memory into the conversation. Perhaps I thought it would be a piton of shared experience on which to hang some form of guide rope for him.

I leaned back in the chair and adopted what I imagined was a thoughtful expression. "You know, back before I decided to go into social work, I went to school in order to become a priest. Catholic priests generally get their masters in divinity, which includes a ton of theology — something I really loved — and psychology, but also the practical aspects of ministry. I was great at the first two, but the third, well..." I trailed off and gestured at myself.

The wolf cocked his head.

"It's difficult to balance being the leader of a congregation with being an awkward mess in social situations."

He laughed. "Okay, yeah, I can see that."

"So, they were nice about it, and we weighed our options," I continued. "One option was for me to switch from an MDiv degree to getting a degree in theology, which would be all that intellectual research and navel-gazing that I loved without the pastoral care I was simply not cut out for."

"But you didn't," he hazarded, gesturing at my degree on the wall. *Master of Social Work, Univerity of Idaho, Sawtooth.*

"I didn't, no. Another option that we discussed was me transferring out of the program and into something else. I opted for that."

"How, though? Why? Like...why would you choose that over the other option or toughing it out in your divinity stuff?"

I shrugged. "It was complicated."

"You're telling me," he said, rolling his eyes.

"I know you don't share my faith, but those are the terms I think of that conversation happening in, so you'll have to forgive me for using them."

He nodded for me to continue.

"In these situations, we call this process 'discernment', wherein you do your best to discern God's plan for you in life. Do you go on to get married? Do you go into monastic life? Ministerial life? Hermitage?"

"And you chose married life?"

My mind flashed to Kay and I held back a wince. I laughed to hide my discomfort. "I chose helping others, which is why I'm here, but God's plan for me was to do so on an emotional level rather than a spiritual one, one on one rather than in a congregation. It's easier for me to be genuine one on one with someone than it is for me to relate to a group. It's easier for me to have a conversation and work out problems together than it is for me to teach and preach. My advisor agreed, and said, *God needs saints more than he needs priests,* which stuck with me."

He nodded, and I could sense a hint of impatience in the gesture. "I don't have God to lean on, though. I'm not sure I believe in any overarching plan for me to reach a goal or whatever."

I shook my head. "No, I understand, that's just the language I was using at the time, but the act of discernment is what I'm getting at. It's not a one-and-done deal. At least, not for most of us normal, imperfect folks. It's an ongoing conversation we have with ourselves about what's important to us and how we get where we want to be."

At that, he relaxed. "Oh, yeah, I get that. Like, I went into school thinking it'd be great to do chemistry and get into, I dunno, materials science or something, and I'm struggling with that. I guess a better way to think of it would be something like, uh...I guess I'm having this conversation–"

"Or you need to," I interjected. "The discomfort may be a sign that the conversation still needs to happen."

"Yeah, I need to continue to work on this process of nailing down what it is I want to do."

I nodded. "And one thing that falls out of that is that you're going to learn more from yourself and maybe things change. There's no harm in them changing, you're just getting new data from yourself about it."

He brightened up. "Yeah. Yeah! I like that."

I like him. I like all of my patients, of course, but he's a good kid, and far smarter than I was at his age.

I was just so sure of myself, back then. I was positive that I wanted to get my BA, learn Greek, then my MDiv, then head back here to Sawtooth and start right away in the ministry. My parents were also incredibly pleased with this decision, if decision it was. It felt like a decision at the time, but now I'm not so sure.

Did I decide to do something that felt so self-evident? Was it just the path of least resistance? I remember when I began to struggle, when I decided leave the program, that conversation with God. I remember admitting it to myself, the confession the next morning, the meeting with my advisor.

But was *that* a decision? Was I giving responsibility to God for an action that I myself took?

These feelings of doubt have been cropping up more and more, recently. I do not doubt in God, but I am beginning to question my relationship with Him. Saying "God knows what is best" is an awfully handy way to absolve oneself from the responsibility for one's actions.

I know it's right for me to not be in ministry. I wouldn't make a good priest. I wouldn't be happy, and thus my congregation wouldn't be happy.

But I don't know if my path here, to this point in my life, has what is required to be called a decision. I wound up in secular life, but I wasn't thinking what that would entail. All I was picturing is that I would not be Father Kimana.

Now, here almost in my thirties, all of the decisions seem so much bigger, even if their impacts are smaller. That's not to say that pursuing Kay would be a small thing. It has the potential to be huge. It just doesn't have the change-your-life-in-an-instant quality that leaving Saint John's did. It would be a process. Admitting feelings, dating, marriage, children...all decisions in and of themselves, all with the potential for failure, incomplete success, or mismatches in expectations.

I should go home and eat. I love my patients — nerds, to the last — and they always get me thinking, but lately, all this rumination...

I should go home and eat.

3

I have noticed over the years that we tend to put benches in the strangest of places. I noticed this at Saint John's, those years ago back in Minnesota. The placement of benches ought to be deliberate. There ought to be some sort of goal in putting them where we do. A bench placed in a park with a careful view across the grass, through the trees, down the street would be ideal. You could look at the kits playing in the grass, the trees moving in the breeze, down the bustling street. Instead, we place them facing buildings along sidewalks.

Or, here at work, we place them facing a parking lot. I know, of course, that this bench is here because it is intended to be a place to wait for someone to come pick you up in our car-ridden town. I *know* this, and yet this bench feels so fantastically pointless. There is one in front of short-term and handicap parking which feels far more apt a place for such a thing, but no, perhaps that was not enough: this one is along the side of the building, facing that overflow portion of the lot that on some days sees no use at all.

There is this occasional fad among certain groups on the Internet, I've been told, of seeking out so-called liminal spaces. I think that the term is ill-fitting. Liminality has a very specific meaning. I do not think that many of the places described as "liminal" that show up on social media and forums on the 'net are liminal so much as abandoned and vaguely spooky. They are not a place between, they are not a place one transits, not a border. They are simply poorly lit or forgotten.

The important thing about liminality, though, is not that a place be forgotten and certainly not that it be in any way scary, but that it should slip and slide beneath your interest. Liminality requires some form of passing through, It needs to be a border that you cross or a place that you enter for the sole purpose of exiting. Abandoned shopping malls are not liminal. A barn, canted awkwardly to the side with age, standing alone in a field is not liminal.

A parking lot is liminal. An airport is liminal. A drive-thru is liminal. These are the spaces that exist only to be traversed. They are the spaces where, should you get stuck in them, you will be struck by the unnerving quality of the experience. They are not places that you visit. They are places that, should you visit — really, intentionally visit — you will feel unwelcome because they resist the very idea of doing so. They push back at you, in some intangible way, and say: "You are not meant to be here."

I am stalling.

It's perhaps a little strange that I seem to get the most out of journaling during my lunch breaks. To me, it feels as though I ought to be doing something so personal and introspective back at home, rather than sitting out on that awkwardly-placed bench in front of the office in that liminal parking lot, but there is something about the discomfort of that place combined with me already being in the therapeutic mindset that makes this the ideal situation.

I am stalling, though, because I know that it is easier for me to get caught up in words than to actually do the work at hand. Perhaps I am in the mind of liminality because this idea of liking someone, of wanting to pursue a relationship, is so new to me.

I have long since acknowledged that, despite my ability to listen actively and to guide patients through therapy, I am insufferable. I do not mean to denigrate myself in this. It is a fact and I am comfortable with my role in life. I am autistic and comfortable with all that comes with that (indeed, it works to my advantage in my professional life as I work primarily with other autistic individuals). I have few friends outside of a professional context. I do not enjoy drinking. I am devoutly Catholic. I suspect, for some whom I met at university, even at the private school before that, that I am out of place for being so 'low' a species in such lofty places as those, for such are the places for the cats and dogs of the world, not a coyote who has, in their mind, pried himself up from the blue-collar professions of his ancestors[3] or some imagined poverty.

Along with all of this, however, has come with a necessary distance from romance and relationships. This is another thing that I am comfortable with. The celibacy that was in my future as a priest was not a thing that I was in any way uncomfortable with, and when I moved on from that life I saw no reason to change that. I do not enjoy the word 'single', because that implies something 'less than' in today's society. I am happy alone.

I have, at various points in life, picked up a romantic twinge, and

---

[3] My father was a farmer from a long line of farmers, and mom was a transplant from out east where, yes, her family had long been farmers.

when I do, I cherish it. I will sit with that feeling and enjoy it, and then I will put it up on some shelf within me to be a part of my life, and yet in some way apart from it.

It is not unlike praying in that sense: God is always a part of my life, and yet is apart from it. I do not subscribe to many of the modern evangelical takes on religion, wherein God is within you and Jesus in your heart, but something more conservative and old-fashioned. God is beside me, perhaps. Above me. He is with me, but not within me.

Another way to look at this is perhaps that these feelings are embers, or the smoldering of paper that has not yet caught fire into a relationship. You can see the faint tint of red crawling along the fibers of the paper, and yes, I suppose that you could blow on it and coax it into something more, but better, for me, to watch it slowly consume the paper, enjoy the beauty of the ember and the delicacy of the ash it leaves behind, and then, once it has gone out, acknowledge that it has left me a new person.

That, however, is not what Kay has done. She has flared into my life as a bright spark. It is not the slow crawl of smolder along paper but the bright flash of magnesium caught fire. Unstoppable. Undousable. Inevitable.

This — this and joking about the fact that that we both have what sound like single letters for names, Kay and Dee — is why I brought her up to Jeremy, this brightly burning light in my life that has suddenly claimed me. This feeling is new. It's novel. I have had what I had assumed 'crushes' were before, but to be smitten is a very new feeling for me, one that I do not quite know how to approach.

Kay and I met during the last year of her undergrad and the first year of my graduate studies at UI Sawtooth. She had taken a job in the campus library to help pay her way through school, working in the interlibrary loan office, a service that I was starting to use more in earnest.

That's four years gone now, though, and that these feelings were not in place soon after we met clouded my judgement when I started to pick up so intense a set of emotions. When one feels a yearning that saps one's strength, one expects that this is to be fairytale-level pining. Love at first sight. Smitten by looks. Utterly taken with the ways in which one speaks.

But no, when I first met Kay, I had made a mental note that she was a conventionally attractive coyote, no-nonsense and to the point, an absent-minded dresser, and almost frighteningly competent. I read in her some of the same facets of an awkward social fit that I see within myself, and I suspect much of her quiet efficiency stemmed from the fact that she, like me, often found herself feeling insufferable. It has taken me training and practice to soften my voice, to understand expressions, postures, and the vocal tics that make up people. I feel myself to be an empathetic person, a fact which drove me first to ministry and then to psychology, but to *actually connect* with those around me on an individual basis took effort.[4]

I freely admit that the ILL office was not necessarily the type of place where one focuses on exemplary customer service, but still, this did not seem to be something that Kay was interested in in the slightest. She was there to do her job, do it quickly, and do it well. After a few visits picking up and returning books[5], I decided that I

---

[4] It still does. It is, after all, called emotional labor for a reason.

[5] More than I needed, perhaps. I had access to ILL as long as I was a student, and I took advantage of it.

would try to befriend her and find out how much we had in common.

Was this some early expression of my feelings toward her? I do not know. I do not remember feeling in any way romantic toward her at the time, yet for me to deliberately seek friendship from someone was not a thing that I might otherwise have done. I do remember thinking at the time that had I asked her to talk over a coffee, that would have carried such connotations, so instead, the next time I had an order of books to pick up, I simply asked her major.

For some reason, I remember that she had been in the middle of typing something when I had asked, claws clicking on the keys, and that she had stopped and blinked rapidly at the screen, and I imagined thoughts crunching out of gear within her head.

"Music," she had said. "Music composition, actually. Why do you ask?"

I shrugged. "I don't know. I just always seem to wind up talking with you here, so I was wondering. You don't seem like one of the salaried employees."

Her smile was wry as she replied, "I'm not, no."

I don't remember if we talked about anything else that day, and there were not any stand-out conversations over the next however many times I saw her in the office, though we soon started talking every time I came by and the few times I saw her in passing both in the library and on campus. At some point, we simply...became friends. I do not know whether we would have done so without me having acted with the intent to do so. Perhaps we would have. I do not remember thinking about intent-of-friendship much after that first conversation, so perhaps all it took was that opening question.

We slid effortlessly into a routine of sharing lunches several times a week. I went to a few concerts with her, though she knew far more about the music being played than I and I often felt in over my head as we listened to the instrumentalists and vocalists on stage. I was surprised to find on the first concert that she wore earplugs throughout. I did not find the music to be too loud, some string quartet, perhaps, but she explained to me that it kept her from getting overwhelmed.

At the end of her time at UI Sawtooth, I had the chance to attend her senior recital, where several other students from the various departments performed a few short compositions of hers. The music was cerebral and, to my ears, dissonant, even dark, but it was as fastidious as her in a way that I cannot explain. I applauded heartily and after the show we hugged and she invited me out to drinks with her family, who all proved quite friendly and much like her. Thinking back, I suspect that must have made quite the sight: four coyotes sitting around a table at a fairly nice restaurant, speaking in essays to expound on whatever thesis has come into their heads.

Spending time with others on the spectrum was not a strange occurrence to me, as I had known a few in university and had as a matter of course of course met several in my training, but for some reason, that night was the first time I could say that I felt comfortable in that portion of my identity. I felt at home with others, and, strange as it seems to say, rather like a member of their family.

My lunch break is nearing its end, out here in the liminal lot, so I should probably hold off from writing any more, but I should note before I do that it *is* interesting that much of what I describe here in retrospect bespeaks an early attraction that I had not at the time attributed to budding romance or anything so grand.

Perhaps it was, in the end.

4

It is a Saturday today and I have no clients, so I am attempting to write at home rather than on a bench somewhere or slouched in my office chair, and am actually using my computer for it this time rather than scribbling on a steno pad. I have to admit that I feel very strange writing like this. It feels almost like a violation of a habit, despite having only been at this for a few days.

I have put some further thought into what I wrote about over the last two days, about the fact that there may have been some hints at romance or a crush or what-have-you prior to the time when Kay moved away.

I do not think that, at the time, I was thinking in terms of romance, and I also don't think that it was on Kay's mind either. Her parents may have been of the mind that we might have been going out with each other, but I do not know.

However, I am also not sure that my conscious self was entirely in line with my subconscious at the time. I speak now in retrospect, of course, and at the moment I know very well that they often float closer and further away from each other in terms of agreement, so I do wonder whether or not my subconscious was heading deeper into a desire for more than friendship.

This means that there are two possible scenarios to consider:

- My subconscious mind was starting to, as a client put it the other day, catch feelings, and thus the situation I find myself in now has a longer history than expected
- The history behind this current set of emotions has some later starting point and the way in which Kay and I became friends

has no bearing on the present other than as an interesting story.

If the former is the case, then I think it is worth some introspection as to what about our in-person interactions might have drawn me to her romantically. As I mentioned, she was frightfully smart. She was kind. She was not unattractive[6], either, and as a coyote, certainly someone who ought to have been in the market for me.[7]

If the latter is the case, however, then I have to wonder why it is that such feelings did not form until distance became an issue, for less than a month after that dinner with Kay and her parents, she moved away from UI Sawtooth to prepare for her masters at UI Boise and our communication moved almost entirely to email and PostFast messages. I know that we tried to call once or twice, but neither of us is particularly keen on phones.

When I speak with my patients struggling with anxiety disorders, one of the exercises that I have them perform after a panic attack is to walk back to when the panic attack started and write down what they were doing and how they were feeling. Once they have done that a few times, they can look for similarities in the reports, and then they can start walking back further from the starting point of the attack in order to discover potential triggers. Knowing those, they can begin working on coping and avoidance mechanisms.

I know that I am trying to justify to myself my work on this journal so far, but I think that this retrospection is part of what I am doing with the project. I am not sure that I want to cope or avoid

---

[6]My judgement must be taken with a grain of salt in this matter, given the situation. Do I hedge? Do I undersell?

[7]I know that many of the more liberal bent are increasingly okay with interspecies relationships, but, liberal as I try to be, my upbringing and my time within the church seem to have set me on the straight and narrow path, here.

these feelings that I'm having, necessarily, but I do want to at least better understand when they began, and by understanding the past, better understand the present.

So, in that spirit, I think the first time I noticed this crush on Kay was perhaps six months ago. I remember having spent an evening talking with her about music, about which she has been slowly teaching me, both of us sending each other videos to watch and counting down from three so that we could hit play at the same time and talk about what we were both hearing as it happened.

After the conversation, I had gone to bed thinking that there was something about that particular interaction that felt oddly intimate to me, and when I lay in bed, instead of falling asleep quickly as usual, I spent a while thinking back to her senior recital and that hug that we shared after. In particular, I was thinking about the combination of the feeling of her cheekfur, soft and dry against my own, and her scent.

The room had had more than enough scent mitigation in place, and I know that the sort of non-scent of scent-block had a tendency to cling to fur a while after having been in a room where it had been layered on thick.

However, while the audience had been sitting still and watching the concert, Kay had been up on the stage for much of the performance, conducting, playing the piano, and speaking about the music she had written and I suspect that that combined with any nerves she may have felt prior to and during the performance must have had her a bit worked up, for she smelled more strongly than I'm sure I did.

I remember laying in bed, breathing shallowly as I tried to recall that scent in its most intricate details. My thoughts became fractal in my weariness and I found myself refining and refining my memories. Did she smell of exertion? Did she smell of cleanliness? Did she smell fresh? She smelled of all three, so what were the percentages of each within her scent as a whole?

I remember feeling a pang in my chest as I realized that I wanted to experience that again. That scent, the feeling of her cheek against mine. I wanted it desperately. I craved that moment, drawn out and extended.

I am no stranger to sexual fantasies. I have had them plenty in my life, and am not ashamed to admit that. Celibacy does not preclude one from having desires, and as long as they do not become covetous, God does not proscribe them. But the thing that sticks with me about this night of fantasizing is that there was nothing sexual about it. I did not fantasize about Kay and I some day having sex, of all the things we might do along those lines. Instead, I fantasized about hugging her, breathing deep, then leaning back and, for some reason, brushing my thumb over her cheek.

I don't know why, but that night, that act picked up a talismanic significance, as though were I to perform the ritual — the hug, the breath, the brush through fur — in precisely the correct way, I might somehow feel a light more intense than the sun wash through me, feel a rush of fulfillment, feel a sense of rightness and completion.

Finally, I remember praying. I remember speaking to God and holding in tension my words to Him and these feelings that I was having. I remember asking Him what this meant. What, O Lord, does it mean to desire fulfillment from another person? I do not want to possess them. I do not want to lay with them. I am not even sure that I love them. I just want to be happy with them, want them to be happy, and yet in such a specific way. What does it mean?

The little voice through which God speaks was silent. I was not surprised — the domain of God's works are not the petty interpersonal relationships between individuals but rather whether or not their lives are lived in grace, and whether or not they strive to bring grace to the world around them.

I was not surprised, but I was, admittedly, disappointed. I try not to be disappointed in the ways of the Lord, of course. It's not His job to solve my problems, and to expect him to do so is silly.

Perhaps I just wanted some guidance.

5

I took Sunday off to focus on church, but I have two things of note today:

The first is that I typed up and sent the previous entries that I have written to Jeremy. I will include his full response to me here:

Dee

Good to hear from you, man! I applaud the work that you've done so far here. I know that it can be really hard to buckle down and get to the actual work of parsing your feelings, but this is really great stuff. I like that you are using the journal entries to get out some of your current feelings that don't just surround this crush, though I also like that you call yourself out on stalling. You have talked before about struggling with emotional literacy, and I have to say, I think you're doing a stellar job of improving on your skills. Keep up the good work and try to employ more of that vocabulary where possible.

One thing I do want to mention however, and don't take this as a knock about what you've got down already, is that I think a great next step would be for you to tackle what it is that you're feeling *now*. You've told a really coherent tale of how you got here, and now it's important that you focus on what you're feeling at the moment. Pry at some of those threads and follow them to see where they go. Here are some questions to get you started:

- You mention your feelings on God not providing you the guidance that you wish you had. I hear you, and I know that can be frustrating. Perhaps one thing you could look into is your own response to your feelings on Kay within the context of your spirituality. Do your beliefs influence your thoughts on her? Do you feel that being a spiritual person has an effect on your relationship to her?
- When last we spoke, you mentioned that you weren't sure that these feelings were "real". What do "real feelings" mean to you? What quality keeps these feelings from being "real"?
- From the outside, you seem stuck. You don't seem to want to push for something more between you and Kay, and you certainly don't want to pull back from her. The next step in this project should be to find actionable paths forward. Why don't you start by simply enumerating options. What could moving forward look like? What might stepping back

look like?

Seriously buddy, this is really great stuff. Not usually what I see in journals, but you've always been a heck of a writer.

Remember to breathe!

Jeremy

This electronic mail message and all attachments may contain confidential information belonging to the sender or the intended recipient. This information is intended ONLY for the use of the individual or entity named above. If you are not the intended recipient, you are hereby notified that any disclosure, copying, distributing (electronic or otherwise), forwarding or taking any action in reliance on the contents of the information is strictly prohibited. If you have received this electronic transmission in error, please immediately notify the sender by telephone, facsimile or email and delete the information from your computer.

Jeremy brings up a lot of very good points and I will admit that I am both pleased that he has recognized the work that I have done already (and that he apparently enjoyed my writing) and also a little frustrated that I still have so far to go. However, I recognize that the latter sensation there is a fallacy and the result of me not being mindful and in the moment. The mind is ever drawn to conclusions and finales, when in reality, this is a process, not an end goal to be achieved. He is very careful in his writing there, in that he specifies that I should "see where they go" and "what could moving forward look like". This is very process-oriented language, and something that I would do well to engage with, myself.

I can also tell that he is gently nudging me away from being hung up on the past. I know that that hug with Kay has stuck with me, and that I have done a very good job on latching onto moments when we have gotten particularly close or that she has shown me a level or quality of attention that has felt particularly fulfilling. It is important to have good memories, but it is also important to not stagnate.

The second item of note is that I had a dream about Kay last night.

Dreams are such nothing things. At best, they represent a means by which the unconscious mind adapts to stressors in order to build up defense mechanisms, and at worse they represent random firings of neurons in the sleeping brain — neurons that perhaps fired rather a lot during the day.

Dreams are such nothing things, and yet to them we pin so much meaning.

I dreamed that Kay and I were back at her senior recital, except that she was sitting next to me in the audience instead of up on stage, and we were watching her works being performed together. We were silent, rapt. The whole audience was rapt. The works were of breathtaking beauty[8] and when they were finished, the applause was so uproarious that she was not able to make it back up to the stage to take her bow. I tried to help her, but she got separated from me and was drawn off.

She did not seem displeased by this, however when I called after

---

[8]Not that they weren't very good at the time, of course, though they were certainly beyond my ability as an active listener, and beauty often seemed not to be the goal. She tried to teach me about them, once, but we are not built the same.

her, I, as in so many other dreams, dreams I'm sure we *all* have, had no voice. I was barely able to manage a whisper, and my muscles grew so weak and my limbs so heavy that I fell over and that's when I woke up.

Powerlessness, separation, falling, these are all common features in dreams, and yet I am pretty firmly in the school of dream interpretation being largely bunk. Sleep is a protective action for the body, and dreaming is just the same for the mind. It is unguided, and serves to provide a break from taxing both our physical and our mental forms.

But we are so hard-wired to read deeper meanings into the mindless mutterings of countless neurons. "What does it mean that she was sitting next to me? Does it mean anything in particular that we were separated from each other? Why did I become so weak without her presence?" I am Nebuchadnezzar seeking my Daniel, not the other way around. There is no one to interpret my mene, tekel, and parsin but myself.

Some part of me craves answers to these questions and so many more, but there are no answers to be had because they are non-questions. They are questions one might ask the sky supposing only that that is where God resides.

The writing on the wall. Hah! Dreaming of someone that you have a crush on means absolutely nothing, and yet it certainly feels like it must mean *something.* It has left me spinning with so much to think about and a lot to feel whether I want to or not.

I did not dream again last night.

6

It's been a few days, and while the dream has not come back, it still clings to me like scent. When laying in bed, drowsy and sleepless I will find myself exploring that space over and over again. Did I touch her? Did I smell her? I know that I was attuned to her presence, but did I even get a good look at her?

I do not know. So much left me in the seconds after I woke up that I'm left with the vague outlines of a plot and so many half-remembered sensations.

Today I am writing because I had therapy with Jeremy, and the skunk and I had rather a lot of time to sit and talk through what has been going on. Strange that I did not start with the topic, despite it being so on my mind, but it felt awkward, cliché perhaps, for me to launch right into, "Doctor, I had the strangest dream."

Instead, I picked up a thread from an earlier appointment that we had had. It feels a little off-topic to write about it here despite having done so already, given that this journal has as yet mostly been about Kay and my feelings toward her, but then, this was never intended to be the sole purpose for it. The goal was for me to use it as a tool to improve my emotional literacy when describing my own feelings. It's why I suggest that many of my clients consider journaling, as well.

The thread we picked up is an old one: I have been trying to sort out my feelings around leaving seminary to head into this field. It's been years now, of course, but guilt is tenacious and difficult to disentangle from shame.

I think the thing that I still struggle with the most is that I left on such a whim.

I do very little on a whim. I plan and organize and I watch and wait until I find just the right moment to act and then I do so, and yet to go from being a seminarian to not in the span of a few short days — the decision was all but instantaneous, and then it was just a matter of paperwork — to this day feels incredibly unlike me.

There are days in which it feels like a dream: not in that I don't believe it, so much as the lack of engagement with the idea beforehand did not give my mind time to prepare and internalize the enormity of what I was doing, and so even these many years later, I catch myself beginning those internal dialogs, setting up argument after argument for why I should leave my chosen path for another, and then with an electric jolt, or the sensation of missing a stair on a staircase, or perhaps the rush of a near accident on the road, I realize that the thing I am trying to rationalize has already been completed: the battery contacts bridged, the step missed, the red light run. I have already left and there is no arguments to be made.

And then, as with today, I struggle to try and justify this decision to myself. I have talked with Jeremy — the skunk is an atheist, but well read in religions — and I have talked with my fellows in the church and I have talked with God. The church would welcome me back to pastoral life, I think, were I to want such a thing, I have not abandoned God. If anything, I have grown closer to Him since leaving the path to priesthood.

But that door nonetheless seems shut to me. I made the decision, however brashly, and there is nothing more to be done. It was the *right* decision, too. It was right at the time and it remains so to this day.

The rightness isn't the problem, it was the speed. It was the ease of the decision. How could I possibly have known that that was the right thing to do? I jumped ship from my path toward ministry and straight into a masters program in psychology. Helpful for providing guidance, yes, but what could possibly have caused me to act so far outside the norm? *My norm?*

It was at this point that Jeremy got a strange look on his face and I stopped talking. He said something along the lines of, "Why are you talking about this, Dee?"

I remember shrugging and saying, "It's still on my mind. I've been thinking a lot about how it is that we know what the right decision is."

"Yes," he replied. "But why are you talking about a snap decision when you can't make any decision about Kay? What's different?"

This was more impactful at the time than it seems writing now. I wanted to roll my eyes and say that this was precisely the problem I was facing, that the problem was that the decision came to me with no forethought. However, a therapist usually does not go out of their way to wrong-foot a client without there being more to the question, and so I motioned for him to continue.

"You are a very deliberate person, there is no denying that. You live your entire life in a deliberate fashion. I think we would both agree that your leaving Saint John's was sudden, yes, but still deliberate." He paused and waited for me to nod. "But when you talk about your feelings on Kay, all of that falls away. You waffle and equivocate and stay put, never moving forward."

"I'm trying, though. That's why I've been writing."

"You haven't sent me your latest entries — no, no need to do so now — but that is what I nudged you on when you sent me the last batch. You're doing good work in trying to put words to what you're feeling and I'm proud of how much you've accomplished in just a few weeks, but none of what you sent me felt like you were getting any closer to a decision."[9]

"I suppose that there is a lack of conviction." I was speaking slowly hunting for words, which Jeremy picked up on.

"Is conviction what is missing?"

"No, you're right. I do have the conviction that I have a thing for Kay, but I am still missing something."

I was not able to come up with the word for it during the session, but I think I have it now: I am missing the *basis* for my feelings. They are not *grounded* in anything. Yes, she's a friend. Yes, we share similarities. Yes, she's attractive and my species and a potential partner.

But there's no real basis for these feelings. All of those things were true when we met. They were all true when we hugged after her senior recital. They remain true today. Nothing has changed in our communications other than them moving primarily online and occasionally over voice or video, and yet out of nowhere I suddenly have this enormous desire for her. Not physical desire — though I would not turn down the intimacy — but a desire for her presence. A longing.

There is a concept that I think touches on this set of feelings, which is that of limerence. As long as I am to work on my emotional literacy, it is best that I start trying to name what I feel. To call what I am feeling a 'crush' feels inexact. It is not puppy love. It is not new relationship energy. It is not lust. It is an uncontrollable romantic

---

[9]Jeremy is a very good therapist, and he has an innate quality to his voice that allows him to say things such as that in a non-accusatory way. It is a thing that I have to focus very hard on when talking with my clients. We rarely want to accuse our clients of doing or not doing something, but strive instead to induce introspection. I would have had to add a "Why is that?" to the end of that same sentence to take the sting out of it, but the he can do it just in normal conversation.

desire.

It is not grounded in our friendship or my attraction to her. It is more of an obsession. A desperate need for her to feel the same way about me. A craving. A pang. A wildness of the heart that is as frightening as it is pleasant.

It is an unmoored, unmooring thing, drawing me ever upwards in lazy, undirected arcs almost — *almost* — against my will, ever closer to the sun.

These are things that I am thinking now that I am on my quiet, liminal bench. I didn't have the words then, on the spot in the middle of therapy, but I will have to bring them up next session.

We talked for a bit longer on the subject, but as the time drew to a close, Jeremy suggested, "I think you should talk to Kay soon. Why don't you see if you can bring up how you feel about her some time before we meet next? It doesn't have to be an attempt to start a relationship or anything. Even just telling her that you've been thinking about her would be a good step forward."

So I suppose that is what is on my plate. She and I talk every day, these days, and so I will have plenty of opportunity to do so. Perhaps I will aim to do so tomorrow, as I'd like to see how I feel when talking to her tonight without bringing this up, knowing that doing so in the future is a hard and fast goal for me.

7

I was not able to do it.

Kay just went to bed after we spent much of the night talking over text, and I just wasn't able to bring myself to bring up the way I feel about her.

It's maddening. I've never been so frustrated by the fact that I felt I was putting on a charade. It is not dissimilar from putting on that mask demanded of me by my occupation and just living in the world but have never had to do with Kay until recently. Why would I have to pretend to be some sort of normal around a friend? And yet here I am, pretending I'm not falling asleep thinking about holding her paw every night.

Holding her paw! What garbage.

I talk with her like I talk with strangers, at least whenever we near this topic. I make a stranger out of myself, it seems, though she has not said anything about the way I have been acting. I reread each message countless times before sending it just to make sure that it is plausibly normal, that I am not in some way tipping my hand, that I am being kind without being intrusive, that I am being invested without being obsessed.

I am not comfortable with this change in myself, but I will continue to work on it.

What we did talk about, however, was much of what I spoke about with Jeremy yesterday, about how I left Saint John's. She knew this fact, of course, we'd talked about it before.

What she did not know, however, was that I had left of my own accord. At some point along the way, she had picked up on the idea that perhaps I had been ushered out unwillingly. When pressed as to why, she said,

5:31 PM Kay

Oh, I don't know. I suppose I had guessed that you were gay or into out-species relationships or something.

My reply:

5:31 PM Dee

Oh goodness, no. Not something I particularly have a problem with, but I can confirm that my preferences remain quite straight and quite coyote.

This probably would have been the best time for me to broach the topic, but I can point to this spot definitively as where I chickened out. Instead, I continued,

5:33 PM Dee

What lead to that assessment? I'm curious.

5:33 PM Kay

I'm not sure. You're a bit hard to read so I took that as there being some sort of internal conflict.

5:33 PM Dee

I think I'm just terrible at communicating.

5:33 PM Kay

Also a possibility!

From there I explained much of what I had talked about earlier, about how I started to doubt my calling, rather than my faith or scriptures, and yet how my decision to leave had come suddenly enough to surprise even myself.

Now that I write this and think about her comment, though, I do wonder: the administration let me go with surprising ease. The attempts to keep me along the path to the clergy were faint at best, and I was able to simply walk away from the vocation with little impact to my standing within my own congregation and essentially no strife from the school itself.

I sometimes wonder: why was this? In a church whose adherents continue to dwindle, why was there so little attempt to keep me around? Was it because of me? Was it because they did not see a fit for me? For someone neurodivergent, outside the narrow spectrum of neurotypicality that they themselves held to so strongly? Surely that is part of it, as I have expressed. Was it because I was a pest, though? Were I to reapply, would I be welcomed back, even if I have better learned to function within society through whatever masking they might appreciate?

Was I preempting them asking me to leave by leaving, myself?

I don't know how I feel about this thought. I will pray on it, of course, but as much as the church is in service of God, I do not think that this is necessarily his domain.

Perhaps I should get in touch with the school, or maybe some of my old classmates.

I suppose this is just what I needed: another impossible social problem. Nearing thirty, I would think that I ought to have grown out of these by now.

8

If I assume that there is some subconscious root of my rising feelings toward Kay, and if I am to continue working backwards from a known starting point, then let me step back from that first recognition of those feelings.

We have countless hours of conversations over PostFast and email. We have fallen into the habit of at least saying hi to each other once a day. Sometimes, that is all the conversation that we have and the rest of our days will be eaten up by work and study, by reading and hobbies; and sometimes we will spend entire evenings talking, listening to music or watching comfort videos in the background while we engage on a more constant level.

Before we both wound up on PF, though, we had been emailing back and forth. We still do, on occasion, for when thoughts require something less immediate, something more structured than instant messaging[10]. Sending each other essays and bulleted lists and long quotations that we have found interesting.

I had planned to dig back through those conversations for my Saturday afternoon task, hunting for hints of yearning among however many thousands of words we've shared. But, as happens, I got caught up in the business of the day. I wrote that entry earlier full on planning this, and then I remembered I had to vacuum the last remnants of winter coat from the floor. Having vacuumed, I figured I might as well use that momentum to clean the kitchen, and while there, I remembered that I needed to cook for the week.

Not all plans were made to be followed to the T, though.

Instead of sitting down at the computer and digging and rereading and reliving — or attempting to — I set myself to mindless tasks through which I could live in memory. I thought back rather than reading back, and I did my best to put words to my feelings at the time.

Kay and I's first lunch together was an accidental affair. During that final year, I was spending my afternoons sitting in on sessions and, towards the end, holding supervised sessions of my own. I

---

[10]I have sometimes considered why this might be the case, and I have two main thoughts on the issue. The first is that email allows for threaded conversations. One can respond to a particular email, perhaps even after the conversation has continued from beyond that point. This also allows one to reply inline, even, interjecting thoughts between points one's interlocutor has made. The second is that, as a self-advertised "mobile first" application, PF limits the width of the text per message to what might fit on a phone screen, even when using their desktop application, and something about reading a very narrow, very long block of text feels like a misuse of the medium.

learned early on that a lack of calories in my system would lead to irritability and an increased difficulty in masking[11] for the sake of my patients, so I began leaving my final seminar and heading straight for the student union for lunch before my first sessions began.

The food there was not great. You grow up on a farm in the northwest and you get used to a certain type of food. Sure, there are plenty of steaks and burgers at home, but you also have a healthy selection of homegrown produce and homemade canned goods. There is little enough profit in the industry for family farms, so my parents saved money where they could by growing what they were able to for the table.

The student union, though, had a limited selection of four restaurants: a burger joint, a bagel shop, a soup-and-salad place, and a Mexican restaurant, all of them chains. The soup-and-salad place was my go-to, most days: they were the most likely to have an interesting selection on a day-to-day basis, they were the most likely to have vegetables other than shredded lettuce, and they were the least likely to leave me with an upset stomach later on in the afternoon, even if they were also the most expensive.

I smile to think back on the sheer number of combo meals I ate there. Half salad — usually Caesar — cup of soup, and square of focaccia, all arranged neatly on a tray. Few of the soups were memorable, of course, but almost none of them were bad. I was willing to accept "consistently okay" food.

I was waiting in line, lost in thought, watching the fox on the other side of the counter scoop lettuce and croutons into a bowl

---

[11] I am well aware of the problematic aspects of masking and would never encourage my clients to do anything that would lead to them being so disingenuous, but it is still a tool that I use at work.

where it would be tossed with dressing, when Kay sidled up behind me and said, "Hey, Dee."

I will admit that the context shift of seeing her outside of the library initially caught me off guard. Always, I had been standing before a counter waiting on one of the employees to fetch my books off the shelf. Always, there had been a barrier between us, a requisite space that kept us apart.

Now, though, she was right behind me, standing closer than any counter would have permitted in the past. I hesitate to say that I didn't recognize her out of this context, for her voice was still the same and I could easily put voice to name in my head, but it took a few seconds for it to sink in that, hey, this was Kay. We had talked. We knew each other.

I had known that she was shorter than I, but I hadn't realized just how much. I could see over the top of her head between her ears. I also hadn't noticed her scent before, at least not to this extent. The library was full of the scents of others, despite the open spaces and constant air circulation, so it was far more difficult to pick out an individual's scent over any other's. Now, it was far more distinct, closer, more present.

It was not unpleasant, of course. She smelled of coyote and femininity and slowly fading scent block. There was no scent of stress, either, something I hadn't noticed had always been present in the library until its absence here.[12]

I realized I'd been staring and snapped to attention. "Kay, hey, sorry. Long morning. Lunch break for you, too?"

___

[12] I freely acknowledge that not all have the attraction to libraries that I do, and that the stress-scent I had been experiencing there could just as easily have been something more universally ambient than related to Kay herself.

She nodded. "Yep. Theory classes first thing in the morning, then work, then techniques in the afternoon. I steal lunch when I can."

"I've not seen you come through here before," I said, handing over my card to the cashier. "Don't think I've ever seen you outside the library, come to think of it."

She shrugged. "Forgot my lunch."

I waited for her to pay and pick up her own tray of food. I remember, for some reason, that she had ordered a full salad with strips of chicken on top.

I also remember that there was no discussion of us sitting at the same table and eating together. This was unusual for me. I struggle to eat around others without feeling hypervigilant over how I must appear to them. Too many frowns for chewing too loud, too many admonitions to slow down. That I would just walk over to a table with someone and share a meal with them without thinking was a strangeness that struck me only after the fact.

We talked a little, though I've largely forgotten about what. I remember asking what techniques classes were, and I remember she asked me what I did for work, but the rest must have been small talk that slipped from my mind.

All I remember is the not-unpleasant sensation of seeing something out of place. Kay belonged in the library. That was the context in which she fit most easily. That she might exist outside, might have a life, might actually be a real person, with real hopes, real dreams, the very real need to eat added depth to her, and while, on thinking back, I'm sure while there was no early hint of a crush, there was no small amount of pride in the small success of having seemingly made a friend after setting my mind to the matter.

9

Kay and I's lunch dates continued throughout that semester. First, it was a simple agreement to meet "sometime next week" for more soup and salad, and from there, it turned into a staple. I would meet her at the library at the tail end of her morning shifts a few days a week and walk with her from the library to our chosen spot of the day. We found out all of the delightful little hidden tables in the student union, away from the noise and commotion surrounding the restaurants themselves.

We quickly switched back to bringing lunches from home, rather than continually frequenting the same four restaurants. It would save us money, and as we headed into lent, it was easier for me to bring my own food rather than simply being restricted to salads and the burger joint's atrocious fish sandwiches.

"Peanut butter and jelly?" Kay asked one day. She sounded incredulous.

"What's wrong with PB&J?"

"Nothing. I just can't picture eating something like that as an adult. It feels like a food I left behind back in grade school."

I lifted a corner of the bread. Sprouted grain bread — that one luxury I permitted myself if only due to its significance — cheap peanut butter, cheap jelly. "I'm not much of a cook, I guess."

Kay grinned chewing a bite of her much more exciting-looking sandwich. She held it out toward me, speaking around her mouthful. "Bite? Ham'n'such."

I laughed and shook my head. "Thanks, I'm alright. It's lent, anyway."

The coyote worked to swallow her bite, ears perked upright and head cocked to the side. "Lent? Like...honest to God, give up something you really like, fast and pray lent?"

It was my turn to chew through the sticky morass of peanut butter, and I had to take a drink from my water bottle to even begin to speak. "Honest to goodness lent, yes. Though I generally stick with the prescribed 'beasts of the field, birds of the sky' strictures, in terms of giving up food."

"What's the point of all that?" she asked.

"It's symbolic," I said with a wave of my sandwich, as thought that would explain it. "Forty days of lent, forty days that Christ fasted in the desert. Forty is one of those big numbers in the bible."

She shook her head. We'd had enough conversations by this point that neither of us was really willing to go down the conversational road of discussing religion. I was Catholic, she was not. On that point, we were immiscible, and at the time, I had no problem with it.

I don't know why the memory of this lunch in particular sticks out to me, though. It was just us, there. Two coyotes, sitting in a solarium tucked in against the south wall of the union. Some renovation or another in the past had left the room obscured, and thus often unused and quiet. It became one of our favorite lunch spots.

Two coyotes sitting in a glass-walled room, a painfully bright blue sky, a blanket of snow on the grass outside. Warm, but sensing the nose-stinging cold a few inches away through the glass.

Why this lunch? Why does this one stick out in my head? We talked about lent more than once. We'd talked about food more than once. Why does this one stick out in my mind?

I remember that the conversation stalled after that, at least for a little bit, and we ate in silence. Kay had brought with her a sandwich larger than my own, plus some little single-serving packet of hummus and some carrots — I remember taking one of those and a swipe of hummus when offered — a packet of chips, and a drink.

I finished before she did. I think that's why I remember it. She finished her sandwich and then scooted her carrots and chips and hummus to the edge of the table, twisted sideways in her chair, and put her paws up on the low rim of the wall where glass met concrete, squinting out into the brightness of the afternoon.

I pulled out some notes to rifle through, but gave up after a few pages, instead just enjoying the sun with a friend. Sitting nearby, listening to her crunching on chips, watching the way her ears would flinch back with each sharp snap of the carrot between her teeth.

A separate memory, a memory within a memory: thinking of my advisor from Saint John's. His fur, when we shook hands, was so much softer, so much more pleasant to touch than my own.

That Kay and I were both coyotes didn't seem to matter, her fur still looked as thought it would feel softer than my own.

I don't know if I'm remembering this correctly right now. I don't remember if the Dee that was sitting in the sun was thinking about whether or not Kay's fur was soft, or if that's just the Dee right now, sitting here and writing about that moment. It's such a nothing memory of a lunch that I can't disentangle the reality from the moods I've been wilting under of late.

I just remember that I gave up on the notes and we both sat there, even after she finished, saying nothing, soaking in the warmth.

10

Our last lunch together took place the week after Kay's senior recital, and after we greeted each other, we spoke little, as though all the clamorous notes and weighty silences from her performance still hung beneath us. We ordered our food separately and it wasn't until partway through the meal that we realized we had ordered the same thing, which drew a laugh from both of us before we focused back out on the lawn behind the student center.

And then, with all the suddenness of applause after a performance, our conversation, our words were ungated and we were free to speak.

"How do you feel about your performance?"

She eyed me slyly, as she always did whenever I used 'feel' language. "Are you asking as a friend, or are you asking as a therapist?"

I shrugged. "I'm not your therapist, Kay, but if you want to talk about your deepest feelings, you are perfectly welcome to."

"I don't know that I have deep feelings," she laughed. "I mean, I feel things strongly, but I kind of wear that all on my sleeve, don't I? That, or I guess I just put it into music, and it's not like that's any more easily understood."

There were several branching questions I could take from there. I had been learning about that of late, of finding the knots within a statement that would most benefit the client by unraveling. I remember being anxious in following up that train of thought. Was I being rude by trying to draw more out of her? I wonder now: was I trying to get closer to her simply by learning more? I don't know.

Finally, I asked, "Do you feel your emotions didn't come through in the music?"

"I don't know, did they?"

Deflection. I rolled with it.

"I feel like a lot of the emotions we don't have words for we wind up putting into art, don't you? Great painters all make works of art that expresses ideas and feelings that don't come across well in language."

"You really are in a therapist mood." She threw a piece of lettuce at me. I set it on the corner of her tray.

"You've been quiet," I hedged. "It seemed like there was a lot going on, is all."

"Yeah." She picked at the piece of returned lettuce, tearing it carefully into shreds and eating them absentmindedly, one by one. "I guess I'm trying to decide if I wrote the pieces out of some academic need or whether I actually put emotion into them. I can't tell because I couldn't read the response from the audience. The applause was always so...I don't know. It was hesitant, like people were trying to figure out whether or not the piece was actually done, but man, when you hear that from the point of view of the stage or as the artist, it's hard not to read that as though they didn't like it."

"Didn't like it?"

"Like any emotion behind the piece just went over their heads, and instead all they heard was noises on the stage."

I waited, silent, for her to continue.

She rolled her eyes. "And here's where you tell me, *No, Kay, they were wonderful! We were just awed by the breathtaking beauty of your music! Stunned into silence!*"

I tilted my ears back and bowed my head a little. "Sorry. I didn't want to interrupt."

She poked the last bit of lettuce into her muzzle with perhaps a bit more force than strictly necessary. "S'okay."

"It *was* good, Kay, promise. I'm not the best judge of music–" She smirked at this, but I continued. "–so some of the music part went over my head."

Her own ears perked up, and it was her turn to wait me into talking more.

"Like, it sounded dissonant and dark. Not angry or sad or anything. It just sounded dark, like there was a lot going on beneath the surface when you wrote them."

Her expression softened and she nodded. "I think there was. I didn't mean for all of them to be dark, though. Some of that was some shitty performances. I had some choice words for some of the performers after."

"I'm not quite educated enough to say one way or another on that." I thought for a second, and then shrugged. "And I don't think I'm educated enough to say whether or not the music was too academic or too emotionally abstruse. It did sound like there was a lot going on, though, and that a lot of that was maybe stuff you couldn't put into words."

She nodded. "There was, yeah. And no reason it can't be both, right? That's what I was thinking about. Some of the emotions I was feeling and trying to put into music were complex, and maybe went over the audience's heads, but also this was supposed to show my talent as a composer, and so I was supposed to write really, uh...academically dense stuff. Show-off-y, you know?"

"So, all that plus your performers lackluster showing, I can see that leading to feeling like it just didn't translate well."

Another nod. She ate the rest of her salad and set the bowl aside.

Still facing the windows, we sat together in silence, watching spring sun draw students out into the grass after a class block ended. A Frisbee appeared. A hacky sack.

"What were the emotions?"

Kay blinked, nonplussed, until the question clicked into place, then laughed. "Oh, you mean the emotions that were too complex to put into words? *Those* emotions?"

"I guess, yeah."

She looked to be on the edge of adding in a bit more snark, but the response appeared to have been tempered, as instead, she said, "They weren't dark. Or not all of them were, at least.""Three Pieces" — that was the one for solo piano, remember? — that one was about music itself, like how there's a signal path from composer to audience."

"Signal path?"

She leaned forward and drew lines with her clawtip on the window. "Sure, like...someone sings into a microphone, right? That generates a signal that goes down the wire to the sound board. You know how it's got the banks of dials above the sliders? Well, the signal travels down through those knobs one by one, then down through the slider that controls the volume, then all the signals are combined into a stereo signal controlled by the master sliders, then it's out through the speakers. Signal path, see?"

"I think so. So, how does that apply to composer and audience?" I could guess, but she was smiling now, excited. I didn't want to take that away from her. Or, I realize now, from myself.

"The composer writes the music — that's the signal — and then puts it onto paper, gives it to performers, who play it for an audience, who take it in through their ears and mix it all up into their heads until they can come out at the end of the piece with a picture of what the composer was thinking or feeling."

I nodded. When she appeared to drift off into thought, I guided her gently back. Perhaps I was greedy for her immediate presence. "And you were trying to convey that through the piano."

She frowned. "Sort of. Not, like, the idea itself, since I obviously just used my words to explain it, but this weird emotion that that makes me feel. Like...there's a little bit of magic in it, you know? So I feel a little bit of wonder at that. But there's also a little bit of responsibility. It's sort of like I'm the magician and have this responsibility to pull off this crazy hard magic spell for everything to go well. Except that's not the whole thing either, because there's also the performers outside my control, and there's all these looping detours between composer and performer and audience, like the process of finding performers, the journey they take learning the music, and then all the techniques and how well they work in the performance space and how that affects how well they work and–shit, I'm rambling, sorry Dee."

"Wait, what?" I sat up straighter and shook my head. "No, Kay, you can talk music to me all day long. I may not be able to keep up with all of the fine details that go into it, but I like hearing you get all excited about it." I followed this up with my best earnest expression and a wag of my tail, adding, "Besides, you're good at listening to me talk about all those things that I get excited about, too."

Her guarded look relaxed into something more like relief, and she wagged a little, herself. "Thanks. It's good to have someone to gush at. God knows I don't understand half of what you say, too, for that matter."

We laughed and began gathering up our stuff, shouldering our bags and piling lunch detritus onto our trays to take to the trash.

A few steps from the trash bins, Kay bumped her shoulder against my arm. At first, I thought she had stumbled or something, and I swerved slightly as my empty drink cup nearly tumbled off my tray. Her expression was curious: she had her ears splayed in something like anxiety or worry, and her whiskers were slicked back, guarding. She wasn't looking at me, and yet she was smiling.

"And thanks for coming to see it, and for drinks after."

I don't remember what I was thinking then.

I don't remember how well I'm remembering all of this. Am I looking back through the past with rose-colored, Kay-shaped glasses? Is my vision bounded by a shape of her that I want to see, and am I trying to fit my memories of her to that shape?

I don't remember what I was thinking, and I remember little of what we did after, other than we threw away our trash and then went our separate ways.

I don't remember if I felt anything then. I want to say that I did, but I see even myself through those Kay-shaped glasses. I see myself back then, a few years younger, a few years dumber, and I see a coyote in love. I see two coyotes in love, flirting back and forth. But now I'm a few years older, a few years wiser, and, as a coyote in love but *also* a therapist, I know that I ought to be careful.

I don't remember feeling in love, and I don't remember if Kay actually had that guarded, bashful expression when she elbowed me on our way to the trash bins. Come to think of it, perhaps I confabulated the whole thing. I remember a lunch after her recital, and I remember discussing signal paths. I definitely made up the bit about tearing lettuce, because I was trying to rebuild the mood of the lunch the better to remember.

But is that a good idea? Is it a good idea for me to try to rebuild a mood when here I am, looking for specific things?

The Dee of today is looking for evidence that he was in love, and, ill-advised though it may be, seeking evidence of the same in his interlocutor. I can't picture that doing anything for this reconstruction process but influencing vague memories to fit expectations. It's all so frustrating.

I don't know if this exercise is even a good idea, now. What do I benefit in learning what I felt before getting a crush on someone that will help in the present moment?

I am unsure of myself, as always. Dewí Kimana, perpetually hedging his bets, perpetually worrying that he's going to put his foot in it after decades of perpetually putting his foot in it. I will keep remembering things, of course. It's comforting to think back on pleasant times with pleasant coyotes. But I am not sure if will keep up this exercise any longer. Maybe I'll save those memories for stupid dreams, and should any leave me reeling the next day, perhaps I'll share those, instead. After all, Kay left her own signal path, from those lunches through the formation of memories, and then years of being tossed and turned, digested and reformed into feelings that lay close enough to the surface that the signal can once again leave my paw and spill out onto the page, and all I can hope is that, as Kay put it, I'm left with a picture of the thoughts and feelings that I might have had at the time.

11

There is a strangely comforting humiliation to the act of confession, to admitting to the one on the other side of that screen just how long it has been since you engaged with your sins so directly, so honestly. You kneel on that delightfully familiar kneeler, the same you knelt on in high school, the same you knelt on when you got home from your failed venture in Minnesota. You fold your hands, you nearly rest your nose against them, doing your best to smell only your scent and that of the cedar before you, not the priest, not the feline who was in there before you. You admit your deeds and the words roll off your tongue with the aspartame tang of your shortcomings.

For a while, when I was getting my psych degree, I stopped going to confession. I will admit that there was a brief time during those studies that I thought I understood quite a bit more than I actually do. I knew enough to be dangerous. I thought, "Ah yes, if confession is the catharsis of letting go of an internal stressor, I needn't go to confession, so long as I have that regular release of spiritual energy!"

But while confession certainly involves catharsis, that's not its sole purpose. I got my catharsis from the class trip to a junk yard where we were given goggles and sledge hammers and let at a stack of cars, from letting a friend talk me into driving up into the mountains so that I could shoot his pistol, even from visiting a batting cage.

But it wasn't the *right* catharsis.

I never felt like I was handling my sins when the bat made contact with the ball, and even when the ball hit me instead of the bat, I still had not served penance. I wasn't shooting my guilt, not blasting away my unworthiness before God. I was just panting and yelping like an idiot in a fenced-in enclosure. I was just tasting cordite or stale oil on the air, not the clean, cool flavor of the act of contrition.

I lacked the post-catharsis cleansing, and so I went back to confession. I lacked the flavor of it.

It is not anything so grand as synaesthesia. I don't think that voicing my sins actually tastes like an artificial sweetness, one so sweet that it hurts your teeth despite the implicit promise that it not do that. It's not an actual flavor in my mouth, just this sense so strong that that is how sin must taste spilling from the lips, that is how confession must taste.

Thinking back, this has always been the case for me, at least when talking about anything of such dire import.

I remember the night I decided to leave Saint John's. I remember leaving the library and walking to the quad, taking the long way home to put off walking alongside traffic on the road. I remember praying as I looked up to the stars, and then as I sat on the grass, and then I remembered that same tang of confession in my mouth as I said to myself, "I don't want to be here."

I tasted that again today, still taste it.

"Forgive me, Father, for I have sinned," is when the taste started. "It has been three weeks since my last confession."

Citrusy-sweet words from a clumsy mouth.

"I have felt desire towards someone..."

Sweet, gritty, leaving the tongue feeling a little too dry.

"...who I am not sure feels the same towards me..."

Salivary glands working overtime.

"...and it is taking a toll on me. I can't think of anything else."

And then, with a few words, the taste beginning to lessen, the words of my priest: "Are these thoughts adulterous in nature?"

"No, Father. She is not married."

"Do they stem from lust?"

I frowned down at my paws. "I don't think so. It is an overwhelming need to be with her, even just romantically. Like I need her in my life."

"Like you need to possess her? Keep her? Do you covet her?"

"Perhaps. Certainly to an extent."

"And what have you done to address these thoughts?"

The crushing weight of my iniquity sliding from the back of my neck to rest on my shoulders. I shrug weakly. "I have been praying for understanding, but Father, I don't want to rid myself of them. I want to fulfill them. I want to be good to her, I want her to be happy. I just also want to be a part of that."

"I see."

"So maybe it is a form of jealousy, or perhaps envy. I'm yearning for something I can't have."

"You can't have that fulfillment?"

"No I just..." I fumbled for words before coming up with, "It just feels like I can't have that, like it's out of reach."

"I see two aspects, here." The voice was quiet, comforting. "The first is that you are lusting for her — and I say lust because there is more to that word than simply the carnal. It has to do with a desire that is out of control, to the point where it truly claims you. Lust and greed can go hand in hand, and both tie into the second aspect, which is that you are coveting something to the point of distraction. You are spending more time thinking about the little lie you've told yourself, that you can't have her, than you are about the world around you. Does that sound correct, my son?"

"Yes, Father."

After a moment's silence, the priest continued. "We all know the commandment that you should love your neighbor as yourself. There is a balance to be struck there, because you still have to love yourself, too. You don't disappear out of these equations just by virtue of loving your neighbor, you still have to attend to your own needs. If you need that love in your life, then perhaps that is worth seeking out, because not doing so only seems to be causing you pain. Does that make sense?"

It stung to have that laid bare in front of me. I counted three long, slow breaths before I replied. "Yes, Father, that makes sense."

There was silence on the other side of the screen, and I could hear a quiet cough from outside the confessional. Words failed me, and a pang of worry that I was being unfair with the priest's time. The tang on my lips was starting to fade, so perhaps I had voiced all I could.

"For these and all my past sins, I ask pardon of God, penance, and absolution from you, Father."

A soft hum on the other side of the screen, that soft noise the priest always makes when considering penance. And then, "Alright, my son. I would like you to say five Our Fathers for your penance. I also want you think on who it is that you're envious of, or what you are jealous of. Think about that balance of loving others and loving yourself, and ask yourself who it is that you are hurting in these situations as you pray."

The weight on my shoulders slid down and off of me. "Thank you, Father."

That was Wednesday, and coming on Friday evening, now, I still do not know the root of my jealousy. I waffle still.

Sometimes, it feels like envy. It feels like I'm craving something that I cannot have, something that is being kept from me in some form or another. By whom? Who would possibly be keeping me from Kay? Kay herself? God? Myself? I cannot begin to place any sort of blame on any one source.

Other times, however, I recognize that there is nothing keeping me from 'having' her, and that perhaps I am simply jealous of something that I do not yet have, but see myself having in the future.

And other times still, both words fail, and I'm left simply with yearning.

I'm left with yearning, and I know that the only one who I am hurting in these situations is me, that to love myself as I would love a neighbor feels always out of reach.

12

I see a client with obsessive compulsive disorder. She has a tendency to pick at her fur and skin, some troubles with physical affection that make her feel 'gross', a fear of driving that leads her to worry that someone has been struck by the car, and a sort of external claustrophobia that leads her to struggle with the idea of closed-in spaces such as cabinets and cupboards, which we suspect stems from some early childhood abuse.

She also struggles with relationship-rightness with her husband. She worries constantly that he might not be, in some way, okay. It's not that she thinks he might not love her, or that she might not be good for him, but that if there is anything wrong in his life in any way, that she must address it. It goes beyond simply needing to comfort him, and well into the territory of her world falling apart should anything be wrong that she cannot address.[13] It did not matter what that wrongness might be. Often, the wrongness would be unnameable, ineffable, hypothetical.

When I brought this up with Jeremy during one of our sessions a few months ago, speaking specifically to the stress that I felt in masking around someone who existed in such a high state of activation at all times, he asked if I had greater trouble masking around those who experienced strong egodystonic symptoms and feelings than those who experienced strong egosyntonic symptoms.

At the time, I explained it thus. Those egodystonic disorders, the ones that impede upon the patient's life, brushing their fur the wrong way and leaving them in discomfort or pain, often lead to high-stress situations where I find myself struggling with the task of expressing appropriate emotions, engaging that visible sort of empathy that helps so much with patients and which I feel I must constantly practice. I find myself wanting to disengage in order to protect myself. Avert my eyes. Cross my arms. Close myself off from the stressors before me.

Egosyntonic symptoms, where detrimental feelings, symptoms, or thoughts do not disturb the patient's sense of identity, are far easier for me to mask around. It feels much more natural for me to try and engage with a patient with visible empathy if my goal is to try and help them understand that a behavior might be damaging

---

[13] I suspect that their relationship is codependent, as I think that her husband gets as much out of taking care of her as she gets out of him taking the lead. However, I don't think that it's abusive or manipulative in anyway, simply that this is the way that their relationship works. If there is any negative aspect to the codependency, that, I suspect, is egosyntonic.

to themselves or others. At that point, masking is a tool in my kit.

I suspect that this habit may stem from my early connection with the church. If an individual sins, knows that it is a sin, and struggles with that, it is far more uncomfortable than if an individual sins, does not consider it a sin, and cannot see the spiritual consequences that they might thus face. With the former, I struggle to mask because it is their goal, their work, their job to find their way back to the path, but with the latter, with the one who sins in ignorance, they must be met with empathy, for they know not what they do, etc. etc.

Ah well.

All this to say that I am starting to come to the conclusion that limerence is the egodystonic form of attraction.

I suspect there must be some similarity to addiction here; the overwhelming pungency of limerence is not pleasant. It is a thing that must be maintained, just as a high-functioning addiction must be maintained. One must have that drink at the end of the day. It feels bad to drink it, it feels bad after, it feels bad to *need* it in order to maintain a functional life.

Similarly, this crush, if that's all it is anymore, requires of me a constant level of maintenance. I have to feed it fantasies, have to pour energy into it. I have to dream, both at night and during the day. I have to imagine the feeling of our fingers intertwining.

It is a negative part of my life in both its concrete and emotional effects. It feels perilously close to sin.

I think that's why I sought out confession. What was it the priest had said? *Ask yourself who it is that you are hurting in these situations.*

I remember the surety of knowledge after that, that the only one I was hurting through these struggles was myself. And now I have better language for that, that this pain is egodystonia. Limerence is something that rankles with my identity, as negative a part of my life as it is. It is a greedy thing, that which has laid claim to a portion of my concept of self, and I object to that claim.

Liking someone isn't a sin. It cannot be, must not be. But here I am, wallowing in my own pain, and that is where I veer close to sin.

Why must we Catholics wrap our every action up in shame? There must be some root for some bad thing in my life. If I am depressed, it must be for some reason, for something that I have done, yes? If I struggle this much for liking someone, clearly there must be something shameful about that, yes? That sense of dread, that sour, ashen taste in the mouth, that is a sign from God that we have strayed from the path he has set before us, yes?

I'm a *therapist*. I should *not* be thinking this way. It's not just wrong, but it reeks of hypocrisy.

Even as a Christian, there is little enough reason for me to think this way. I have read my Ecclesiastes. I have read my Job. I have buried myself in those words, in Job's speeches and of those of his friends. I have dug through the arguments on theodicy, I have written my essays, taken my tests on the reasons for bad things happening to good people, how not every terrible experience has its roots in sin. I *know* these things.

At least, I thought I did.

I don't know. I'm spinning my wheels, talking in circles. I don't know what to do. I don't know where to go from here. To name a feeling may be to understand it, but understanding has gotten me nowhere, has purchased me nothing but a deeper ache in my gut, and now I must feed my desires all over again.

13

Often times, when I work with a therapist (from either direction), we converse quite freely and with essentially no friction. I do not know whether that's a thing that therapist-clients engender, necessarily. I've had my fair share of clients who were incredibly easy to talk with. Not that they're likeable, or at least not only because of that, but that our sessions — me and those clients, and me and my therapists — tend to move forward with a sense of purpose.

In my clients' case, these ones in particular are there *for a purpose*. To get better, to understand their trauma, to do the work. Not just take a pill[14] or do the meditation and be cured of depression, but to really understand it, unravel it, and wind it back up into something new, something neater than before.

In my case, I am here to do the job of improving myself and Jeremy is here to do his job of guiding me along that path.

My path of improvement, as I suspect must be the case with many of my colleagues, is to cope better with the process of taking on others emotions. A good therapist has to have empathy, after all, and I do try to be a good therapist. We don't simply let emotions slide off of us in order to be some impartial observer, we have to feel a little bit of what our clients are feeling as well in order to truly work with them.

So it is that most often, I work through processing the residual trauma of the past two weeks' clientele with Jeremy. Sometimes we'll get onto something that goes a bit deeper, digs further into the past, though perhaps less often than he would like.

---

[14]Not least of which because I am not a prescribing doctor.

Lately, though, we've been spending more time talking about Kay and, along with that, the friction between us has grown.

I started to feel it in earnest today, and, being the good little therapist that I am, I took a step back and examined my feelings and brought that up with Jeremy: "I feel a little sore that I'm being pushed on this."

Every time I get all therapist back at him, he smiles, which I think I secretly enjoy. He replied, "Why is that, do you think?"

"I think I worry that this isn't real work."

"How would sorting out your emotions not be real work? I think that was one of your stated goals."

"Maybe it just doesn't feel like a real problem. It feels like a very intense emotion that I'm not feeling for any particular reason."

He nodded at that. "You mentioned last time that it feels outside your control."

"At least more so than any other emotion that I've worked on before." I thought for a bit, then added, "Or maybe 'outside my control' isn't quite right. It feels purposeless, in the same way depression might. I like Kay. I think about her a lot. We were pretty good friends for that year, and still are, but this sudden intense desire doesn't seem to come from anywhere. It just kind of showed up and now it's slowly taking over."

"Did you wind up talking to her about this?"

"Not really, no."

"How come?"

There was a silence as I sifted through my thoughts. Despite their intensity, they were difficult to pin down, as though too much lens flare obscured the exact source. "I find myself thinking often that I don't want to say anything to her because I don't want her to feel pressured to reciprocate."

"That's her decision, though, you can't take that away from her. Has she had a problem setting boundaries before? With you or in general, I mean."

I laughed. "No, not at all."

Jeremy grinned, but kept on pushing. "Then is that wholly true?"

"I'm not sure. I just don't want her to feel obligated to feel the same way about me that I feel about her."

"Projection, maybe?"

"I'm not convinced it's *that* baseless."

"What is the basis, then? Have you felt pressured into saying yes to someone you didn't want to say yes to before?" he asked.

"I'm not sure. Perhaps. I know that going into seminary was not originally my idea. I liked it there. I believed. I felt myself faithful enough to wind up on that path. Still, it was my parents' idea."

He nodded. "And you felt obligated to go along with the idea?"

"Yes."

"So perhaps a bit of projection." He raised a jet paw to forestall my disagreement. "Both things can be true, Dee. It can be projection, and it can also have some truth to it."

"Alright, I'll concede to that."

"Projection in cases like these often stems from a difficulty in being vulnerable."

I winced.

"I know that being vulnerable isn't something that comes easy to you. You are an earnest person in general–"

"Sometimes it feels like I have no other choice."

"–but when it comes to specific situations, you come up against some internal resistance. Have you been able to be vulnerable around Kay before?"

I nodded and recounted our conversation about leaving Saint John's.

"That sounds like a good bit of forward progress, then. Do you have any other things that you could be vulnerable to her about?"

"How do you mean?"

"Well, if there are a few topics around which you have trouble being vulnerable, perhaps you can work up to them. I still think that it should be an end goal for you to talk to her about your feelings, but that doesn't have to be something that happens right away. You can practice, first."

And so now I'm thinking: what more do I have to be vulnerable about? I'm a thirty-year-old coyote with an awkward social manner, a strongly-held sense of faith, and an otherwise simple lifestyle. My past is unremarkable. My future holds no surprises.

Am I really so boring? Do I really have so little to worry about? Am I that privileged? An uncomfortable thought. It makes me feel shallow.

And yet Jeremy is right. The friction surrounding this particular vulnerability is too great for me to overcome just yet, and I am still not convinced that this feeling is real enough that opening up is something that is even worth doing.

Instead, I wonder if the right thing to do is just to focus on being a good friend. I do not know if this is something that I can ignore, *per se*. That isn't how limerence works. It is an intrusive thought. It is something that bypasses whatever safeguards one might set up to sidle up next to you, press itself close, and whisper wickedly into your ear: "You need them. Doesn't matter how, doesn't matter why, but you need them."

I don't know if I can ignore it, but perhaps I can use it as fuel. I can use it as a spark to just continue to be a better friend for her. A better listener, a better support, a better Dee all around. Am I not to practice my emotional literacy? Can I not use this as an opportunity? Transmute limerence into personal growth.

We will see.

14

I feel compelled to state that I do know the *reason* that I left a path to pastoral. That was something that I talked through with my advisor at Saint John's, and something that I had been struggling with for a while. I can point to it and name it as the mechanical reason. What I don't know, necessarily, is the reason why I left there in the way that I did.

I left my MDiv behind because I do not do well in front of a crowd. Simple as that.

Put me in front of a person, and I can have a conversation with them[15]. Set me loose in a crowd and I am fine. If you set me down in the middle of the 13th Street Plaza in the middle of the dinner rush or in downtown Boise and watched, I suspect that you would see nothing out of the ordinary.

I don't say this to brag. Rather the opposite, actually, The recognition that I do okay on the street in the middle of a crowd because, after a certain point, I cease being able to see the people around me as real people and the weight of their presence no longer weighs on me, and just how *low* a number that needs to be before I cannot

---

[15]I would make a terrible therapist if I could not do so.

keep up with individuals is embarrassing. Three people I can manage. Four is a stretch. Staff meetings are difficult.

Drop me on the altar in front of a congregation and expect me to connect not just with the congregation and its constituent parts but also with God and I get lost before I can get started. If I were able to focus on just one of these things, if I were able to look out over the heads of the parishioners and see only cardboard cutouts of ears and snouts, moving in time with the liturgy, I would likely be able to do that — I gave my fair share of speeches. If I were able to participate wholly in the divine rite and wrap myself in the mystery of tradition, I would be more than happy — I have my fair share of rituals.

But that's not what mass is. Mass is connecting the congregation to God, and that means being the conduit between the two of them, and that I *cannot* do.

I recognized this early on, before even applying for Saint John's, and set my mind specifically on powering through this deficiency. I was able to learn so much, could I not learn how to provide communal spiritual interaction?

Alas, some things are intrinsic and immutable. I left because I recognized this fact. And so, it turns out, did my teachers.

I bring this up because work[16] asked us all to provide presentations in our weekly staff meetings, something which the cynic in me explains away as "prove that you're paying attention and doing your job to higher ups and call it a 'brown-bag lunch'."

Fine. Whatever. I can write a little speech. I rather liked the

---

[16] I work essentially as a contractor. I run my own practice, but under the umbrella of an organization that helps handle payments and parcel out clients to the member-therapists.

practice of writing speeches and homilies in school, and if the style in which I journal is anything to go by, I still very much do.

I don't mind the writing, I just mind the thin sheen of bureaucracy that colors everything about dealing with my employer, sometimes.

15

I have volunteered for the first of these 'brown-bag lunch presentations' and am not shy to admit (at least, to myself and Jeremy) that I did so simply to get it out of the way. I have little desire to participate in team-building exercises in the context of an organization that exists solely to facilitate one-on-one interactions in a professional context.

My thoughts on this whole process are clear, so I shall not complain any further.

I have decided, as it is occupying my mind of late[17], to talk about discernment and the reasons that I am where I am now and not wearing vestments. I already even have the example of my client who is going through his own form of secular discernment.

To that end, I have been toying with the balance of life story to academic content, and have decided to lean perhaps 80% of my presentation on individual stories (both mine and that of a few anonymized clients), and then set that within the framework of psychology.

The core idea of what I want to share, I think, is the importance of taking one's time to make decisions, as well as to understand the unavoidable malleability of those decisions and long-term plans.

---

[17]I mean, alongside Kay, but I am *not* giving a presentation on Limerence.

The things that decide the outcome of long-term decisions may, after all, be long-term problems. You may, for instance, be a stupendously awkward coyote trying to wedge himself into a position of social grace that requires absolute earnestness and humility.

I have been collecting notes about my own process of discernment, as well as examples of discernment in others to pull together into this speech:

- The client who is struggling with his choice of what he is majoring in at university.
- My parents' decision to marry (and thus dating as a whole).
- Having my dreams interrupted by a sudden recognition of reality.

I think that this is enough to get across the point of taking a long-term decision-making process into account in a therapeutic context[18]. I don't have to give an academic lecture or provide any references, of course, just offer some thoughts from what has come up in and before my own practice.

On further consideration, despite my thoughts on the context of this presentation, I think it might actually be fun to write the essay that will underlie my speech. It ought not be all that different from what I am doing here, after all, right? I am providing myself with a forum in which to voice my ideas, explore them to their conclusions, and learn something along the way.

I emailed Jeremy my thoughts on the matter, since he works for the same organization that I do and will doubtless have to give his own brown-bag presentation at some point, and this was his response:

---

[18] And besides, I am a sucker for lists of three.

Dee,

Yeah, that sounds like a fantastic idea. I was about to caution you about the difference in tone between a speech and a journal entry, but given what you have shown me so far of your work, I don't think that that's necessarily a worry for you. I think I've told you "you think in complete sentences" or some variation on that enough times at this point that it has become almost a cliche 😺

One thing that I think I would suggest is that you write this 'journal essay' ASAP so that you have enough time to get your thoughts out of the way. You've mentioned before how easy it is to get caught up in your own thoughts on something while they evolve in the middle of you trying to share them. Write your presentation, then maybe journal about it some, get all the thoughts out of the way that you can so that you're not distracting yourself at the front of the room.

Good luck, buddy!

Jeremy

No harm in that, I think. I'll get those words down and maybe even spend the night before rehearsing them, just to be safe, and then try and make it as fun as possible for myself, and hopefully that will come across to the audience, as well. Might as well try to turn corporate bullshit into something useful for those who have to put up with it.

16

The presentation went over quite well, I think. There were a few questions after. Jeremy said it sounded good and my boss thanked me in a way that was more than just a *pro forma* thank you. Some part of me wishes that I had offered something less personal, but the rest of me is just glad it's over and that I don't have to care about it too much going further.

For posterity (and an admittedly uneasy sense that I ought to attach just about anything to do with this current task of journaling to the journal itself), here's what I wound up writing:

> Before I set about the task of working toward my current career, I was on the path to becoming a Catholic priest. I made it all the way through my BA in religious studies and a year and a half into my MDiv before figuring out that it just wasn't going to work, and that I would make a terrible priest.
>
> The reasons for this are fairly simple and also not necessarily germane to what I would like to talk about today, which is the process of discernment. Built into the education and administration of running a seminary, even the whole church, is a set of safeguards to help members onto the paths of life that are actually best for them, even if it isn't what they originally thought. This is set down explicitly in the term "discernment", which St. John's University, the seminary that I attended, codified into a system used by the administration.

A cynical way to put it would be a filter to keep the bad priests out, but in reality, it was a way of drawing out a decision that should — or must — take time to commit to. Some decisions are just not meant to be made quickly, whether or not this is because they are bound by time constraints, or simply because they need a lot of thought.

I got started thinking about this in a therapeutic context by a client recently. He was struggling with his decision to pursue the degree program he had chosen at university. Something about it just wasn't clicking for him, as much as he liked the idea of it. During a session, I brought up discernment as a topic that can be extended beyond its ecclesiastical roots and into just about any decision that requires time to play out.

I described the process of making this decision as an ongoing conversation with yourself as we find out what's important to us, what it takes to get where we want to be, and what is within our reach.

I'll note that that last bit is not actually something I said out loud to him. Whether or not he is actually able to pursue his degree to its conclusion is not on me to decide, I don't know one way or the other, but it stood out to me as something that I had experienced.

You all know that I'm a very awkward person. It takes a lot of energy for me to have a conversation with more than one person and to engage with those that I am talking to in an interesting way that doesn't leave one or the other — or both — of us frustrated. Can you picture a priest struggling with something like that? I may have had a mind for theology and all that goes into the bookish side of being a priest, but I don't have it in me at all to do all of the *other* work, most of it based around social interaction, that goes into the calling.

This is what I mean by discernment. In the context of the church, you take a long time to settle into a path that you will stick to for the rest of your life, whether that's a pastoral role, as a member of an order, or simply as a parishioner, but the same can hold for just about any other long-running decision-making process.

My advisor at St. John's told me that one could think of it like dating. The process of discernment is one of figuring out the relationship between yourself and a potential outcome of that decision before committing to what may be a mistake.

That can even be very literal. My parents dated for about two years before they decided to get married. In the context of their social lives and their families, this was an absurdly long period of time, but something about each other just made them want to be extra, extra sure that they were ready to be together forever. It's not that they were at each other's throats or constantly frustrated with each other, either. They were some of the most in-love people I've ever known. This year would have been their fortieth anniversary, and until the day they died, they were still holding paws and giving each other these little fawning glances.

Where my decision to join the clergy failed, that's an example of a decision that worked out well in the end. Extremely well.

Neither my client nor I know where it is that he will wind up. That is still a decision that is underway. But ever since having that session with him and making the connection between what I had gone through in the past with discernment and the idea of slower decision-making processes, I have made a conscious effort to keep this in mind when working with all of my clients who are struggling with big changes in their lives.

The discussion afterwards was fine. We talked a little bit about other long-term decisions that therapists had run into — things like divorce, changing careers, and so on — as well as some other personal stories. It only lasted a little bit, but since it was time taken out of our normal shared lunch break, no one was eager to stick around, least of all myself.

Again, corporate nonsense.

I shared a bit of this with Kay and she sent me an eye-roll emoji, followed by

6:03 PM Kay

It's bullshit like this that has me glad I'm still in academia. Not that libraries are immune or anything, but they're strange in that you're either a page or assistant like me or you had at least a masters degree.

6:03 PM Dee
I have a masters.

6:06 PM Kay
Well, fair enough. Still, I think libraries have this ivory tower nonsense going on in ways that places like you work don't. Reference librarians stick to their subjects, book binders stay in the bindery, book purchasers buy books, assistive tech people deal with assistive tech, etc etc. There's no real effort to bUiLd a TeAm in the same way as it sounds like is happening with you and every other office drone I know.

6:06 PM Dee
I'd shake my fist at you for calling me an office drone, but you're not wrong.

6:06 PM Kay
I bet you dress in business casual.

    I laughed and typed back:

6:07 PM Dee
Of course I do! Have to look professional after all.

6:07 PM Kay
Do you call it "biz cas"? If you do, I will block you immediately.

6:07 PM Dee
I do not, thank goodness. I call it a button up shirt and slacks like a normal person.

6:08 PM Kay
You are absolutely in no way a normal person.

6:08 PM Kay
What did you wind up talking about anyway?

    I sent her the essay and then waited for her to read, feeling anxious, as I always seem to when sharing anything related to religion with Kay. She's never been anything but kind-but-disinterested when the topic has come up before.

Finally:

6:12 PM Kay

I mean, it sounds like a fluff presentation.

6:12 PM Dee

It was hardly an academic conference.

6:13 PM Kay

Yeah, but it's not really -about- anything, I guess.

6:14 PM Dee

I guess, yeah. Just a loose compilation of thoughts. I wanted to be the first so I don't have to worry about any presentations for a while.

6:14 PM Kay

Hahaha! So cynical, Dee! Never knew you had it in you.

6:14 PM Kay

Especially given this apparently pretty earnest speech.

6:15 PM Dee

It was earnest! I am cynical! I contain multitudes.

6:15 PM Kay

Now I'm just picturing you as a priest.

6:16 PM Dee

Black cassock and Roman collar? Or all the vestments for mass?

6:16 PM Kay

Oh, the black one. Total hot priest vibes. You just have to wear that and call everyone "my child" or whatever and the girls will be all over you.

Gears crunched to a halt in my mind. I must have sat there, staring at that message, for several minutes, trying to parse out just how much of it might have been serious.

6:21 PM Kay

Sorry, that was probably pretty insensitive...

I rubbed my paws over my snout before replying:

6:25 PM Dee

No no! Just never really thought about "hot priest" being a thing.

You're just not on the right parts of the internet.

The conversation wound down from there, so now I'm writing up my journal and turning Kay's words over and over in my head. They fit strangely into my image of myself. 'Hot priest'? 'Girls all over me'? There isn't a universe in which either of these things is true. I am no judge of how attractive I am and have never bothered to ask, but the idea of a priest being sexy makes my head ache. They are two completely separate concepts in my mind, a Venn diagram with no overlap.

And having 'girls all over me' just sounds unpleasant no matter how I take it. If I can't deal with more than three or four people in a room at a time, how would I deal with that in some situation that might suggest intimacy? And in the more idiomatic sense, well, I can't even deal with attraction towards just one girl.

17

It is Pentecost Sunday. It's still a Solemnity, but after Holy Week and Lent, it lacks anywhere near to the same level of impact, so although the mass differs from a mass during Ordinary Time, it lacks the social impact of the other holidays.

I always find myself using it as the marker of slipping back into Ordinary Time. It works well for me to treat it as a very deliberate point. It is a relaxing of posture, perhaps. A time to switch from the tense contrition of lent and the jubilation of Eastertide into the, well, ordinary ritual and everyday faith.

Another interesting bit of news is that, as of last night, I appear to be taking the week after next off and heading up to Boise to visit

Kay.

Like so much of late, the decision to do so seems to have sprung, fully formed, into my mind. Or perhaps our minds, as, when I mentioned the idea of coming up to visit, Kay responded readily and eagerly.[19] She mentioned that there is a percussion festival being held at UI that she would like to go to, and that she would welcome a concert buddy.

"Besides," she said on PostFast. "It's been ages since I've seen you."

If I were in any other mindset, I think I would have taken this at face value, just as I'm sure I would have taken so many other things from our conversations over the last however long. Then again, if I were in any other mindset, I am not sure I would have suggested a visit.

I'm not, though, and I did, and now I am panicking on Pentecost. Was it some tongue of flame that descended upon me, caused those words to come tumbling out onto the screen, enter key hit far before I'd really allowed myself time to process the request? Was it some inspiration beyond myself, or something within myself? Perhaps my subconscious desires are acting out for me.

But now it's set. I sent in a note to work and, assuming it is approved tomorrow morning, I will send out emails to my clients to inform them of my time away and my phone number to call in case of emergencies — and perhaps work can set up remote sessions if they would like — and then start considering what I will pack for a few days vacation.

I emailed Jeremy, and he replied quite quickly from, I assume, his phone:

---

[19]A fact which I am striving not to think of as a big deal.

Wow! Big step there. I was going to caution you about putting yourself in a situation where you would be pining away all the harder but a. You're a big boy now and can certainly handle that, and b. It might actually do you good to be assertive about the things you want in life. Do you think you will talk to her about your feelings while out there?

J

I haven't yet replied, as I am stuck on what to provide as an answer. The question itself made my stomach tie itself in knots. We, Kay and I, interact so smoothly over text that the thought of saying "Hey, I think I really like you" face to face makes my anxiety spike.

I mean, it also spikes when I think about telling her over Post-Fast, but certainly not as much.

So I guess I have yet to decide what to do about that, and instead of trying to figure that out right now (or all at once, as I keep telling myself), I'm focusing instead on what we'll do. She says she's found a few good inexpensive restaurants around the area, and, as I suspect that I am more comfortable financially than her, I will perhaps take her to a nicer one, maybe on the night of that concert. She's also promised to cook at least once and says that she's not bad at it.

There's also the percussion festival, which, on the surface sounds fun, if loud. I like drums well enough, though I imagine it won't simply be drum sets on a stage. Maybe we can fit in a hike or something?

Weirdly, though, the thing that I'm most interested in out of all the ideas that have crossed my mind is just sitting in the same room with her. Even if we're just reading or relaxing on our phones or, as always, showing each other videos that we enjoy.

Less than just doing *stuff* with her, I'm more excited about simply being around her and existing together. That feels like a good 'friend' thing to do.

It also feels like a couples thing to do, but on introspection, I feel like this particular desire may be more bound up in friendship than limerence. It has been a very long time since I have just hung out in person with someone whose company I enjoy.

I have the bus ticket, I have a few room-rental options I am looking at.[20]

All I need is to make it until then.

18

I will not deny my excitement for this upcoming visit.

Neither, apparently, will my subconscious, for I have had not one but two dreams since our agreeing to visit, and given that it has only been three nights since then, this makes it a majority of my time spent thinking about her.

The first dream was much like the one I wrote about a few weeks back. I was at her senior recital, it was unspeakably beautiful, and then when I tried to help her up onto the stage, I was pushed away by the crowd, unable to call out to her.

In fact, it was so similar to the first dream that I nearly did not write about it here, but the very act of sitting down at the desk to

---

[20]She made no mention of me staying with her, and even if I trusted myself to do so, she has shown me pictures of her place before, and a studio bedroom with an extra bed would be quite cramped.

write seems to have dredged up all of the subtle differences.

Yes, the music was breathtaking, but in an almost hypnotic way. The audience wasn't simply listening to it, we were enchanted.

Yes, the applause was uproarious, but it was outsized, for though the audience was perhaps a few dozen people in that intimate auditorium, the sound of the applause was of hundreds, thousands of people.

And yes, the applause was well earned, but more than that, it sounded possessive, as though at the culmination of the concert, the audience wanted nothing more than to claim Kay for their own.

And finally, yes, I did move to help her up onto the stage, but the act was one of desperation, as though that was not simply to help her take a bow, but to rescue her from the grabbing hands that wished to take her.

I didn't just fall away out of weakness, I was actively pushed away, I was an impediment on the audience's way to claiming what was rightfully theirs.

As with any such dream, this all felt astoundingly normal. It was not a nightmare, at the time. It was just a dream in which all of those things — the enchanting music, the audience, the possessiveness — were simply an inherent part of the universe. They were a core truth. They couldn't *not* have been present.

And yet, two days on, the anxiety of having Kay taken away from me (such as it were) clings to me like scent-block. I can feel it as an oily residue in my fur, between my pads.

The other dream is...I don't know. I have only been up a few minutes, now, and I am still struggling to internalize it. The part of me that is able to interpret is not yet functioning, though I have my coffee already, but the part of me that desires interpretation has been online since I crawled out of bed. I do not know *what* the dream was, certainly not what it means, but I suppose the least I can do is write it down.

I dreamed that, during the visit, we were sitting down on a couch to watch a movie and that Kay surprised me with a kiss. The dream jumps from there to us in her bed, trying to...it is hazy. We were trying to make love, and it's not that anything was wrong or necessarily preventing us, not in the dream's universe, but my point of view kept rewinding back to the point where we had just lay down together. After a few of these "rewinds", I found myself — not the me who was laying down, but the me who was dreaming, or perhaps observing the dream — getting frustrated with the repetition, and I started to change up my approach. What if I put my paw *there* this time, instead? What if I kissed first instead of touching? What if I lay on my back? What if I lay her on hers?

It was one of those fruitless dreams of struggling to find the *correct* way to engage with an idea. It was an erotic dream, but without the catharsis of orgasm.

I don't know. I am just as sure that my feelings for Kay go far, far beyond sex as I am sure that I would not turn down sex, should the topic ever come up.

If I'm honest with myself, given my current struggles over even telling her that I have these feelings for her, I think the idea that I actively pursue sex at any point soon is not just inadvisable but outside the realm of possibility.

I just don't yet know what it means.

19

It's been a few hours, and I have decided that that dream was simply the process of anxiety over the trip combined with a spike in libido. In the other, yes, I could see the layers of meaning going on there, with the ideas of possession and being shut out, but when it comes to what amounted to a sex dream with little in the way of plot or inherent meaning, I don't think there's much one can draw from it.

It all feels a little silly, being anxious and horny. I'm in my 30s, for goodness sake.

20

I have packed all I think I will need. Laptop in case of emergency appointments, books, steno pads, toiletries. I have clothes enough for a week, including my blazer and slacks for when nicer clothing is required. Kay did not specify the dress code for the concerts, but better safe than sorry. Also, perhaps we can head out to a nicer place to eat one night.

Here are at least some of the things I've thought of as ideas for stuff to do, so that I can at least have them written down somewhere:

- Concert — Kay obviously already requested this.
- Movie? I don't know what's out at the moment.
- Nice dinner. Boise has to have a good place we can go.
- Hiking. This will probably depend on whether we can find some way to get to a trail when neither of us drive. The maps shows a small nature reserve that's just on the edge of town. I imagine that will be fairly accessible.

- Bookstore. This may be more for me than her. I do not need any more books, but that will never stop me from browsing.

I think that this will at least give us a good number of options, and we can play the rest by ear. Even if we wind up doing what we do on the regular, just showing each other videos or watching movies together, only co-located rather than over the 'net, I will be happy. I stand by what I wrote before, that just being together, even if that's 'being bored together', is quite enough to look forward to on its own.

It's weird, though. I find myself tiptoeing around these different ideas of what to do while I'm out there, thinking things like, "Is this a thing that just friends do? Is it weird for friends to suggest going to a nicer restaurant?" They are all lies. They are all protective actions. They are all me guarding my soft underbelly to keep from exposing my feelings to Kay. Of course friends go to nice restaurants together. Of course that's a thing that friends do. And even beyond that, trying to hide the fact that I desire more than friendship, at least on some level, is doing neither of us any favors.

I am such a coward. Lord, give me the strength to be honest for once in my life. I know that the petty request of a petty coyote is far outside Your purview. What worth is an intercessionary prayer for something so trivial? I am responsible for my own growth, it's my own failing here.

I never did decide whether or not I would be talking about my feelings with her while I'm out there, and I never did message Jeremy back.

I can tell I am just going to keep fretting around in circles if I focus any more on this. It is so easy to find some way to fractally manage expectations, to forever refine what goes into making a plan, to find ever more layers of meaning in an action, and I will (apparently) do that for hours on end, so I am going to set all of this aside and go for one last walk before bed in an attempt to wear myself out. The bus leaves early tomorrow.

21

Boise is much as I remember it. Sprawling, flat. The trip up I-84 is familiar enough to tug loose memories from when my parents would take me up every few months to see a specialist,[21] only now there are far more billboards and what used to be strip malls have turned into tumbled collections of big-box stories, imposing, half-rendered amongst the landscape of scrub and crumbling roads.

I did not miss it, and it seems indifferent to my return.

Kay is still at work for a while yet[22] and I cannot check into my rented room for another few hours, so I have camped out in a café in the neighborhood where I will be staying.

I cannot put my finger on what exactly feels so different about this place from Sawtooth. There is a different tension in those around me. The landscape is similar enough, but there are more buildings, and they are situated just a little too close together, compared to what I'm used to. There is more exhaust in the air.

But it's still Idaho. We're only a hundred and change miles up the road from Sawtooth. The water tastes the same. The tempera-

---

[21]I don't remember what it was for, in particular, and my parents never talked about it once I got older. I think they may have been concerned about a learning disability. I only remember heading up to a house on the outskirts of town, talking for an hour or so while I played with toys on the floor, and then we would go get food and head home. It was a two hour drive, and I would usually sleep on the trip back. I wish I could remember more of it.

[22]The library, natch.

ture is the same. It's all more of the same. Not just in the sense of the ongoing homogenization that is part of living in the west, but it really is no different than Sawtooth, other than it's bigger and more expensive.

It was the bus ride, perhaps. It was that liminal seat, half-reclined. It was the window with scrub grass and cows and small farms blurring past. It was those two hours and the knowledge that I would be *elsewhere* that put me in the mind of differences.

I suspect that I will feel out of sorts for a little bit, yet, at least until I meet up with Kay.

After all, it could also just be lingering expectation.

22

I met up with Kay an hour or so after I checked in to my room — enough time for me to shower and change clothes. The sent of the bus still lingered in my nose, but that may have just been my imagination.

I wish I could say that it was some joyous reunion, but instead, it was just as though we had picked off from where we had been after our chat the night before. We said hi to each other without fanfare and simply walked to dinner. She had picked out some sandwich place that she said she frequented for lunch[23] which was perfectly acceptable fare.

Afterwards, we walked around a nearby park. Perhaps by virtue of how well-tended it was, it was something of a shock to be dropped

---

[23]The part of me which has been so focused on memories writing this journal teamed up with that part always on the lookout for hidden meaning to make me wonder if this was an intentional callback to our shared lunches back in Sawtooth.

into green after all the drabness of the city and the brown of the landscape before that. I will not deny my pleasure briefly cutting through grass to walk beneath trees rather than just padding always along sidewalks.

We walked and we talked.

At first, it was awkward and somewhat stilted as we subconsciously renegotiated our interactions with each other in the embodied world. It is easy enough to chat or not when one is bound to a screen. Even voice-only communication is different when one can mute oneself, or only be heard when hitting a key on the keyboard.

The immediacy of interacting in person, however, brought with it all those scattered silences, filled pauses, and other dysfluencies. It also brought the universal problem of where to look. Do I look at my interlocutor? Do I look at the ground, the sky, the trees? Do I acknowledge those others we come across?

I am so terrible at this.

Eventually, though, we fell back into old patterns. Despite our daily conversations over text or voice, there was a surprising amount to catch up on once we both opened up again. Kay spoke about her time in her masters program, how it differed in structure from her undergrad, the ongoing struggles of finding others to perform her works. I talked about settling into my practice and how I was able to get my full license, about my patients (anonymously, of course), and about my own therapy.

Despite this catching-up, the conversation was all so quotidian. I can't think of any other way to put it, but we just talked about "normal" things. What else could we talk about with each other?

I suppose we could talk about feelings, but walking through the park on the very first evening that I was there, looking forward to a week of time in close proximity, such as it were...well, it did not feel like the right time to bring any of that up.

I am unsure of how to process this first night just yet. The anxiety that I was feeling beforehand, as well as the slowly unwinding tension as we began to speak more freely seems to have taken much of the worries about my feelings for her off my mind, and I was simply focused at first on recalculating what level of masking[24] was required around her, and later on the sheer mundanity of our catching up. I am left wondering what that means, if it means anything. Perhaps it is a habit thing — we fell back into our usual patterns — but more likely it means nothing. We're friends, we talked like friends, and that's it.

I did at least learn that she's single, so there is that.

23

Kay has taken a few days off of work while I am out here, but we wound up intentionally leaving plans fairly loose.

I do not know her reason for doing so, but if I am honest, I left plans open ended because I was not sure what we are, or what our dynamic would look like until I arrived here. Are we just friends? Are we on to something more? Is it weird for friends to go out to a nice dinner? A movie ought to be fine, but should that influence the genre?

I wrote yesterday that we were friends, that we talked like friends, and that that was it because that might indeed be the dynamic of our relationship, I still must contend with these strange

---

[24]The hypervigilant psychologist part of me cannot stop thinking in these terms, and the part of me striving for emotional connection loathes that.

and awkwardly shaped feelings for her. I cannot say whether or not it would be weird for me to suggest a nice dinner for the both of us[25] or going to see a romantic film because I cannot say whether or not this unavoidable set of emotions will make it so.

Either way, I have my list of suggestions and she has mentioned that she has a few ideas of her own, so I suspect that the open-ended nature of our plans won't lead to excruciating boredom or anything like that.

Today went well enough, on that note. I slept in, knowing that she would do the same, and stopped by that same café once more for a leisurely coffee and pastry while I waited for her to text me that she was up and about. She gave me the address of her building and the door code to get in, as well as a coffee order, so I topped up my drink and picked up hers in order to head over. It was a pleasant enough walk, as the day had yet to heat up.

She greeted me at the door in a wrinkled tee and pair of shorts, smiled sheepishly at her unready state, and gestured me into her apartment.

It was a single rectangular room: bed in one corner, desk against the wall next to it, breakfast bar separating the kitchen from the rest of the space, not so far removed from a dorm room, minus the fact that she had her own bathroom and closet rather than being forced to share with others.

A rumpled bed, a messy desk.

And the almost overwhelming scent of *her*. I made it two steps

---

[25] The fact that I am working full time in a reasonably well-paying position while Kay works in a library to fund her living expenses while taking out further student loans means that I fully intend on paying for most everything while I am out here. I really hope that doesn't make her feel awkward, or, heaven forbid, like I am trying to buy her attention. This is all so difficult.

into the room and my mind ceased to function. I might as well have grown talons and wings, for all I know, for all I could do was stand there, coffees in hand, and try and blink away memories and too-strong emotions. I remembered her scent as though a lingering thing, faded touches cheek to cheek within my dreams. I remembered it, but I did not remember its strength, it's depth, it's overwhelming *her*-ness. It was inescapable, unavoidable, permeating and so much more than any lingering dream could ever hope to encompass.

It's a wonder I was able to hand her the correct coffee.

I must have had some strange look on my face, as part way through the sip of her mocha, she tilted her head and lowered her cup.

"Everything alright, Dee?"

I raced through the masking checklist, realized that my whiskers were bristled almost uncomfortably far, my ears were laid flat, I was blinking rapidly, and my tail was tip-tapping about anxiously. I immediately felt an overwhelming sense of guilt, which I did my best to hide behind what I hoped was a bashful expression. "Yeah, sorry," I managed.

She frowned all the same and put down her coffee, padding over to the window to wind it open a short ways. "Sorry, maybe should've sprayed some block. I bet it stinks in here."

"No!" I said, realized that sounded forceful, and added, "No, sorry. Just smells like you, is all, and I feel like I got punched in the face with memories from school."

At that, she laughed, though she did leave the window open, a trimmer chattering below marring her scent with traces of exhaust. "Well, good ones, I hope. Still, I'm sorry it's such a mess."

"It's fine, Kay, really. Just random memories–" *Tell her, tell her, tell her,* some part of my mind was urging. It had Jeremy's voice. "–like going to concerts, or your senior recital." *Tell her!* the voice shouted, pounded on the walls, clawed at my insides, all while half-truths spilled from my lips.

And then, the moment was past.

"Oh! Speaking of, there's two nights of that percussion festival, but I figured we'd just hit up the one tomorrow." She reacquired her coffee and crawled back onto the mussed-up covers of her bed, gesturing me toward her desk chair, the sole other piece of furniture in the studio. "The final night is always the best, because all the stressful master classes and such are over, and everyone is just playing like crazy and really feeling it. At least, that's how it always is with me and festivals. The days are all filled with classes and the evenings are concerts, and the last one, you're just riding on some weird music high. Uh...sorry."

I had leaned back into the computer chair, which had creaked under my weight, and peeked over at some of the papers on her desk — impenetrable sheet music, for the most part. "Sorry? For what?"

"Just rambling, I guess."

"Goodness, no, you're fun when you ramble," I laughed. "I guess I got kind of awkward there, sorry, didn't mean to pry through your papers."

She relaxed back against the wall and let her shoulders slump, holding the coffee in both hands now, tail relaxing from where it had curled around protectively. "Right, yeah. Sorry. I have some folks at work who very visibly lose interest."

"I'm still interested, promise." I smiled as disarmingly as I could and made an attempt to focus through the scent that still tickled its way through my mind.

"Well, thanks," she said, smiling lopsidedly. "I feel kind of weird because, like...um. I mean this in a good way, but I kinda forgot how awkward you are, and remember that I'm awkward as hell too, and that I can just be my awkward-ass self around you 'cause you're always listening at a hundred percent or whatever, and if you're uninterested you'll just change the subject and..."

She trailed off and averted her eyes over to the kitchen, focusing on a wayward glass. All the last had come out in a rush of justifications, half-apologies, and self-deprecation.

"You're fine, Kay. I've gotta be the world's most awkward coyote, and if you're the second most awkward, well, we just make a heck of a pair."

She puffed out a breath and then took a long sip of her coffee. "Mm, right. I'm out of practice in being around someone as...I don't know, genuine as you."

It all tugged at my heartstrings, and I prayed for the bravery to reassure her. "You seem kind of anxious. Everything alright?"

"Yeah, I'm just jittery, I guess. Nervous."

"Nervous about anything in particular?"

She squinted over at me. "You've gotten good at your therapist voice."

I laughed.

"Nah, I don't think so," she continued. Another sip, and then, "I'm realizing how boring I am, and I'm anxious that I'll bore the shit out of you while you're here."

"There's no pressure on my end. We could watch videos online for a few days like we would do anyway and it'd still be a vacation for me."

"I mean, I wouldn't turn that down either." She grinned. "I just don't have anyone around here like you, so I just kind of do my own thing which is not much."

The rest of the day went smoothly. I remember fairly little of it. We got food. We walked to the library and she showed me around. We walked around the campus. We picked up dinner and brought it back to her place where we watched videos as we might have done on any other night.

I remember very little of the specifics, other than the feelings of the day. The feeling of glowing over her words, *someone as genuine as you* and *anyone around here like you* sticking with me as thoroughly as her scent.

24

I am struggling to internalize just what went wrong tonight.

Today was fine. We spent it mostly just dealing with lunch and then poking around for food at a supermarket in case we wanted to cook later. Snacks were also lacking at Kay's so we grabbed a few.

From there, we headed to the percussion festival, which was a short bus trip away. The auditorium was a work of wood fabric panels set into a horn shape, panels all angled in slightly different directions for some acoustic reason that I could not figure out. A pretty, if chaotic structure.

Kay, as I remember from our time in school, brought along earplugs which she put in shortly before the concert started.

I think I struggled with that the most, in some way. I know that she did so to keep from getting overwhelmed, and I know that she did it with every concert, but with all of our conversations leading up to the night along with the fact that she did so well before the music started, it felt as thought I was being shut out. She put in her earplugs and focused on the music all night long, and it was as if, for her, only the music existed.

I am sure that it was some form of active listening on her part, if there is such a thing with music. Analytic listening? Something along those lines.

And yet it was so strange to go from making each other laugh to absolutely no contact with each other, other than the fact that we were sitting next to each other. I should be respectful of her style of engaging with music. I know that, of course. Just as I should be respectful of the concert and the performers there.

It was just so sudden. I ceased to exist, for her. I became a non-entity stuck in a place entirely out of my element.

The music appeared to be perfectly competent. There were rhythms that I could pick up on in the majority of the works, and occasionally a melody that I picked out that fit with my expectations for music.

This should not bother me. It shouldn't bother me at all. She has shown me countless recordings of pieces as strange as the ones I heard tonight, and back when we were in school, I attended several concerts with her of varying quality. Even when my feelings about her began to build, I never really had a problem with our shared silences during performances (such as they are, during a shared video stream).

It never has bothered me, and so why did it tonight? Was it something we did before the concert started? Grocery shopping and lunch? What about that could lead to such a reaction? Was it the reminders of lunches from the past? I'm not sure of that, as we had lunch yesterday and there was no such attachment. Was it the domesticity of going to a grocery store together? Am I attaching meaning to something so mundane?

And even now, it's not as though it was so sudden and surprising as I make it sound. Before the concert, we had to show our tickets, we had to file into the concert hall and find our seats. It was all so hushed, and slow. It was all as I remember it, really. And we did talk, too. She explained some of the pieces she recognized from the program, one of which she promises she had shown me before (though I didn't remember it from the name and composer alone). Afterward, she talked plenty on the way home, and I listened to her gush about the music she enjoyed and complain about the music that she didn't, and while I listened, some part of me was growing more and more frustrated, almost resentful.

Why am I like this?

I don't know what to do with this information, and I think it bothers me *most* at one level of remove. I felt shut out, and that is irksome on its own, but what really bothers me is that I felt bothered in the first place. I felt so bothered that I bent memories when writing this, and only on rereading them did I realize that I was doing so. I'm bothered that I am apparently so fragile as to be set on edge by perfectly normal actions.

It's things like this that set limerence in an egodystonic light. I hate it. I *hate* that I like her and then get envious of the fact that she is enjoying something without me, something that we don't share.

Resentment! Envy! Over what? What do I not possess that I wish that I did but her? And how idiotic is that?

I hate that I feel this way, and then I hate myself for building up so much resentment at myself. No matter the layer of remove, I feel like I fucked up.

I almost wrote "I think I might go home early" but I really don't think that I will. I am confronted with the fact that things will never live up to the ideal that limerence demands, and it has me frustrated, but not so much that I'm going to pull some overly dramatic nonsense like that.

I'm just glad that there are no more concerts while I'm here.

25

I am up early again, and while I do feel better, I am also still feeling tender, and feeling cautious of that tenderness. I want to poke and prod at it. I want to explore its boundaries as one might find the limits of a bruise.

I know better.

At least, that's what I tell myself. I know better than to keep poking at a sore spot, so to that end, I'm digging into the other topic that Jeremy has been nudging me to explore, that of my discernment and sudden veering off the pastoral track and over to wherever it is that I am now. It's been years now, since I left, and although I may just be poking at a *different* sore spot, it is at least one that I know I have work to do around. There are memories there, might as well do the CBT thing and think back to what happened, and then back before that.

It's weird the things that you remember, though. Just little things.

I remember blinking my eyes rapidly in the middle of that meeting, for some reason. It's habit I now know that I have, and once I learned of it, I noticed just how often I do it. I found myself thinking back to all of the times that I had done in it in the past, and there are a few stand out examples that stick in the mind as particularly embarrassing.[26]

I remember blinking rapidly there, in the middle of that meeting, yes, and I remember Rev. Dr. Borenson leaning forward, rested his arms on his desk, and fiddling with a pencil. "Mr. Kimana?"

"Sorry, Father." I frowned down at my paws. Paws grown soft, that far away from home. Some part of my mind, the part always focused on making comparisons, realized how slender and small they were compared to my advisor's big canine mitts, soft from a life of academia and ministry. "I think I was expecting a different reaction."

The Saint Bernard shrugged. It was an informal, almost bashful gesture coming from him. "I'm just not surprised. This doesn't feel like it's coming out of nowhere."

"I have no plans of leaving the Church."

"Of course, Dee. I have no doubts as to your faith."

"But...?"

Borenson sighed, set the pencil down. "Your studies are fine. Better than fine, I'm told. Your teachers speak highly of your writing. That's only half of the program, though. You came here for an masters of divinity, and the end goal of that program is ministry. Your skills in scripture and apologetics, in books, are admirable, but would make for an incomplete priest. We've talked before about you heading for a masters of theology instead, but you balked at that."

I canted my ears back, gritted my teeth, and masked his frus-

---

[26]I suspect there is some reason that such embarrassing things stick in one's own mind while slipping so easily from others'. Perhaps it is a symptom of culture, or perhaps it is simply part and parcel of existing in the world.

tration as best I could. "With all due respect, Father, my concerns about a Th.M stand. Yes, I'm sure I'd be helping the world with research and writing, but I need something more immediate. I need to help people. I don't think I can *not* do that. And there's just too much...I don't know, remove, I suppose, if all I'm doing is writing."

There was a pause as Borenson seemed to manage some equal frustration before he spoke. "Mr. Kimana, an education such as this requires both flexibility and devotion. Both a Th.M and MDiv would require that. Now–" He held up his paws as if to forestall a rebuttal. "I am not accusing you of lacking in either department at least not to a level where I feel you are not a good degree candidate, but if the doubts in your head are strong enough that you feel you need to leave, I would only be doing your future vocation a disservice by trying to make you stay."

I dropped my gaze once more. I spread my fingers, tracing with my eyes the subtle grain on the pads of my paws, the long-healed callouses.

This remains a constant in my life, this sort of discussion. I will research and research and research, come to a conclusion, and when I state what I have learned, the conversation would go sideways. Both me and my interlocutor will wind up frustrated and stressed with no discernable reason why.

But this hadn't been a researched thing, had it? I remember it being something like three in the afternoon, and I'd started this train of thought the night before at, what, eleven? Sixteen hours was hardly the amount of time required to come to a conclusion about leaving behind a year and a half of study and however many thousands of dollars of scholarships that had involved.

No, this idea had leaped, fully formed, into my head.

I focused on ensuring that my mien expressed the sincerity I felt within. I was frustrated, yes, but also confused and more than a little disappointed in myself. "I'm sorry, Father Borenson. I understand. You're right, too, I suppose, that I don't quite have the amount of conviction I'd need for this." The word 'conviction' stuck in my craw, I remember that.[27] "Not conviction, I guess. Something to do with ministry. I don't do groups."

"I mean it when I say I'm speaking from a place of kindness here, Mr. Kimana, but this doubt is mutual. You have a brilliant mind and faith enough, but by virtue of you doubting your vocation, we are all but obligated to doubt you in turn."

I sighed and slouched in my chair.

"If you're not comfortable switching to a Th.M, perhaps it's time to consider switching focuses," the dog said gently. "Perhaps Saint John's just isn't the best fit for you."

"I get it," I mumbled.

The Saint Bernard looked cautious, waited for me to continue.

"I mean, I get what you're saying. I think..." I swallowed drily, straightened up in my chair. "I think I agree, too."

There it was. There was the admission. I'd said it at last.

My advisor visibly relaxed.

"I know I said so before, but I just want to make sure; you know that this is about my vocation, not my faith, right?"

---

[27] I write these memories like a story. It is an occasional dalliance, and I do not quite know where it formed, but it has been with me since youth, to the point where teachers often suggested I major in creative writing. I did consider it, I will admit, though I know it isn't something my parents would necessarily have condoned. Whether or not the words I write here are an exact replication of the conversation that took place is neither here nor there; whether or not I am accurately remembering the emotions that took place is unimportant. I am writing for me now.

Borenson barked a laugh, before his expression softened. "I'm sorry, Dee, I shouldn't have laughed. I believe you. You are one of the most devout students I have. Your decision about your degree may not have been a total surprise to me, but if you had said you were leaving the church, I think I would have called for a doctor."

I smiled, I remember. I smiled through my shame.

26

When I was in school back at Saint John's, I was met with a sudden cessation of chores. I had things to do, to be sure. Things that were repetitive and at times menial, but when you grow up on a farm, the concept of 'chore' goes well beyond simple repetitive, menial task. My callouses have long faded, but during my first months there in Minnesota, they still scraped against my notes and the pages of books every time I interacted with them.

Even when I was getting my undergrad at UI, I was regularly back at home and working. I spent the requisite first year in the dormitories, but went home every weekend to help my parents out. Summer was as full of work as it had ever been growing up, and when my second year rolled around, I stayed living at home, preferring the daily commute — long though it was — to central Sawtooth from the farm out past the outskirts.

My parents were pleased, of course. Help was help, and they certainly loved me.

In Minnesota, though, there was no farming. No hauling, no driving, no commute beyond the walk from my simple apartment just off campus to the campus itself. I quickly developed a walking habit to at least feel some of that same energy expenditure as I had back home.

However, there is a difference of mindset between all the tasks involved in growing soybeans and that of walking. Those chores before may have been mindless, but they required an active enough focus so that one didn't mess up whatever it was one was supposed to be doing. It was goal oriented in a way that walking was not, and the undirectedness of action with walking became a form of prayer.

Well, not prayer, *per se*, but contemplation. It was something more and less than prayer. Sometimes I might begin with prayer, but before long, words would leave me, and I would be left with the sights and sounds, the presence of God. It was beyond prayer. It was beyond meditation.

I'd walk through the campus at night. I'd walk around the Arboretum. I'd walk along the shore of the lake to the smaller chapel, so like the parish back home, so unassuming next to the wildly flamboyant abbey on campus.

And while I'd walk, I'd talk to God. Not pray to Him, not meditate on His perfection. I'd send my mind soaring out over the reeds and the water and taste him on the sickly-sweet scent of honeysuckles. I'd tramp along the wooden walkway in the Arboretum and hear him in the thrum of the boards beneath my feet.

He would be in the bitter, biting cold of February, lingering on the fog of my breath.

He would be in the muddy slog of spring, the indecision of seasons a lazy finger on the scale.

He would be in the way the Minnesota night hung heavy around me, the air as loath to relinquish the heat of day as the year was to give in to autumn. Nearly eleven, the long hours of evening managing to pull away some of the warmth, and He would be in the breath of cooler air coming off the lake. Mosquitoes drifting lazily beneath the trees, and He would be in even that high whine.

Sawtooth has nothing on that.

Here, I will occasionally take a bus or get a ride to the edge of town and walk and hunt for that same quietude that I felt before. I have come close a few times. I came close when I got out past the highway and into the farm lands and walked along the narrow shoulder of the road, watching the sky dip from blue down through salmon to purple, with that brief stop at red that bathed the soy and wheat fields in light like wine. At that moment, I lost all thought, lost all direction, lost all action and gave myself up to the contemplation.

For a scant few minutes, I was able to touch on that space once more and it was there that I was able to talk with God once again.

I did not ask Him for anything — intercession is for the saints.

I did not tell Him anything — He knows all I could ever possibly tell Him.

I do not share the same relationship with the Trinity that protestants do, but at that moments, I suppose I felt some of what they do with their personal relationship with God, with their idea that He dwells within them in some intimate, immediate way.

He passed through me, suffused me with His light like wine, and in that moment, knew me completely, and I could gaze on Him in faith, and I could sit in that silent love.

I stood a while in the gloaming, and as that moment left me, I let it go. What could I possibly do to hold onto God? What could a sinner like me do? How could I possibly hope to ask Him to stay with me? Me, a coyote, a farmer's son, a scraggly beast who failed to live up to his own dreams of pastoral life.

I walked home. No bus, no ride. I walked until the pads on my feet bled.

27

I had to stop, yesterday. I had to stop writing.

I don't know why that memory left me in tears, paws shaking too much to write. I don't even know why I decided to commit that memory to this journal. I started this project with the goal of trying to suss out my thoughts and feelings surrounding Kay, and yet I keep writing about this. I keep writing about God or the Church or leaving Saint John's. I know that I said I would, yes, but it still somehow feels like a trespass.

I walked around the block afterward, trying to calm down, breathe deeply, be present. I did all the things I tell my patients to do when they panic, and I suppose some of it worked. I was at least able to look at the ground, look at the sky, look at the grass and trees and buildings and not feel this unnamed emotion.

If I had any doubt that Jeremy was right in suggesting journaling, I think it has been well and truly dashed by now.

This feeling, then. It is somewhere between shame and guilt. It has that bitter-savory flavor to it. It makes my fur feel clumped and matted. Why have I changed so much since leaving Saint John's that I cannot talk with God as I used to? I do not feel forsaken by Him, I really don't. So why do I feel so much...less in His sight than I did before?

Today, though, I am going for a hike. Kay has a meeting or something at the university[28], so I am taking advantage of her absence to get a bit of walking in by myself, here in a new setting.

28

It turns out that the house I'm staying in isn't far from a patch of wilderness. I do not know why it is called the Military Reserve, but I am not going to turn down the chance at walking away from the city. Boise is so much taller, so much louder than Sawtooth, I feel hemmed in here.

It wasn't quite close enough to walk, but at least there's ride shares.

It's strange how easily I fell back into old habits. Perhaps it was the writing I did last night, or perhaps it's the need to get away that drove me up into the hills, out on a walk, out to blister my feet and talk with God. It didn't seem to matter how unfamiliar the trail was. I just started walking through that scrub and brush, through all that brown and all that air, and not five minutes in did I feel my mind empty, as always it seemed to. The scrub around me, buffalo grass and sage and yarrow and bitter cherry, gained depth and clarity, stalks and crenelations arching up to me, up to God, assuming that is where the heavens live. The colors called out to me. The scents stung my nose, even the five-and-some feet up from my point of view. Bitter, aspirinic whiffs of yarrow. Stale shortcake grasses. Ungreen, but not unalive. The taste of dust lingering on my tongue, not enough to be gritty but enough to remind me that the earth was the earth and that I was separate from that. The air, the air it-

---

[28] And we always knew that it would not be just constant time together when we planned that.

self pushed its way nosily through my fur, a breeze from the west, toppling down off the hills. The air and the hard-packed dirt of the trail beneath my feet knocking vibrations up through my shins. Soft padding, soft crunching, soft rustling; wind in fur, air wandering between tussocks; breathing slowing, calming. Rhythms on the scale from footsteps to seasons.

Even writing this, even sitting on a fence rail at the trail head, I can feel it still.

And through it all, the Lord. Through each and every step, dancing along every brittle stem and blade of grass, surrounding every grain of dust in a blanket of the utmost attention. His voice traveled along the breeze, His breath was the bitter yarrow and shortcake grass. And all of it I could feel and all of it I could hear and all of it washed over and through me and I bathed in it. "His light like wine", I wrote yesterday, and that wine filled me today, and I can still taste it.

There are no conclusions from God. There are no favors that I, a servant, could possibly ask of him. What would He do? Would He tell me what to say to Kay? All He has for me is grace and forgiveness. That is so much more than any other individual could ever offer me.

All the same, I listened for hope, for guidance, for the discernment than hasn't left me since I left Saint John's.

To ask that grace, that breath, that light like wine what it is to do is the wrong question. To ask from Him the worldly answers is to misunderstand the scope of things.

To say that He has no plan for me, no path, however, isn't correct either. He does, and that's why I talk with Him. It's perhaps less than Catholic of me, or at least of a more mystical bent than ought to be expected of me. I'm no Beghard, no Eckhart.

All I know is that sometimes words fail me, and that the Ground does not.

I don't know if that path leads toward Kay. I just can't see that far ahead on it. I don't know if it leads me any further into the Church. That's around some corner I can't comprehend. I don't know anything, it seems, but I needed this. I needed time with myself. I needed this walking conversation, this inside-out hesychasm. I needed out of Boise and away from Kay, away from the scent of her, away from the way she presses against my chest from the inside. I need

29

I know that I stopped writing of a sudden yesterday. I ran out of words, and didn't know what it was that I needed to say that I needed. I just sat for a while, closed my notebook, grabbed another ride back to town, and sat at that coffee shop I visited a few days ago, drinking an ice tea and looking at nothing, and then I went back to my room and sat on my bed and read for a bit. I'll meet up with Kay tonight, I'm sure.

I got my notebook out to see if I could finish what I started, but I couldn't. It's just not there anymore.

Instead, I just dived back into memories. Of that night, I remember first of all the way I cupped my fingers over the bridge of my muzzle and pulled down gently while pushing my snout up. The isometric stretch served to highlight every bit of tension within my neck, and as I held the pressure, I closed my eyes, counting the knotted muscles. Pressed, pushed, and held until I could feel the lactic acid burn deep in the tissue, and then released. With my targets thus marked, I ducked my muzzle down and slid my paws back, fingers kneading along sore spots.

Not for the first time, I wished that I could simply disappear within the written word. Wished that I could relinquish the very idea of physical sensation and surround myself in successive layers of scripture, commentaries, notes. Wished, most of all, that I could wrap myself in the warmth of my faith.

If, at the end of time, faith and hope are to fade, there would be a final sense of completion, but until then, my faith was a comfort.

I shook my head to try to clear the clinging rumination, closing the book of Pauline commentaries and the notebook that I had been attacking with a highlighter and pen.

Standing from my rickety chair, I stretched toward the ceiling, claws brushing up against the off-white-towards-gray paint momentarily before I leaned to the side to loosen muscles in my back.

If there were any one place that I belonged, it had to have been there. There in one of the study rooms in the library. There were books here. There was the quiet contemplation of knowledge, the surety of faith, and the heady scent of aging paper.

And, of course, far fewer people.

I had five minutes until the library closed, which, I figured, was enough time for me to return the book and start the walk back to my apartment without needing to endure any encounters with security sweeping the stacks for lingering students. Sure enough, the only other person I encountered on my way out was the page who numbly accepted the book at the returns desk. A wordless exchange; no small talk, not even a thank you.

The Minnesota night hung heavy around me on that walk back. The air seemed as loath to relinquish the heat of day as the year was to give in to autumn, but now it was nearly eleven, and the long hours of evening had managed to pull away some of the warmth. Mosquitoes drifted lazily beneath the trees, leading me to keep my ears canted back, lest they take interest.

Saint John's University was a lopsided circle nestled at the north edge of a narrow isthmus between two lakes, a marble set over a gap it couldn't hope to pass through. It would be easy enough for me to walk straight north to the apartments along the road that bisected the campus, but I preferred to put off walking along a road as long as possible. The noise — even if the noise was only in the lights around me — was too much.

Instead, I headed east from the library, walking bowered sidewalks for as long as I could. Past the utilities building, past the bookstore, until I hit the quad, that almost-rectangle of grass and trees and sidewalks pinned in the middle of campus. Only then did I turn north, walking through close-cut grass instead of along the sidewalks.

There, at last, I could look up and see the stars.

My steps were slow, contemplative. It wasn't a meander; my walk still had purpose. Instead, it was a putting-off of the inevitable. The inevitable time when I would rejoin walking along the road. The inevitable moment of stepping into my dimly-lit apartment. A delaying of engaging with the real, physical world as long as possible.

Here, at last, I could look up and see the stars, could drink in God's majesty, could forget that I was myself, that I was a coyote plowing through both my scholarships and degree on nothing but momentum. I could forget that I was Dee, and get lost in my total and complete insignificance.

I could walk and I could pray.

Come, Holy Spirit, Divine Creator, true source of light and fountain of wisdom! Pour forth your brilliance upon my dense intellect...

It was here — here in the open, and back in the library — that was where I was most comfortable. Most myself.

Dee, the awkward coyote. Dee, who forgot to smile sometimes, who always seemed to say the wrong thing. Dee, with his nose forever in a book, forever in *the* book, reading and re-reading to tease ever-deeper meaning from scriptures he'd read a dozen times before.

...dissipate the darkness which covers me, that of sin and ignorance. Grant me a penetrating mind to understand...

Was that not why I was there at a seminary? To study and learn? To glean more from the word of God? To live in an ever more Christ-like fashion?

Could I not best learn how to do so there? Was that not why I was there?

...a retentive memory, method and ease in learning, the lucidity to comprehend, and abundant grace...abundant grace in expressing myself...

I couldn't do it. I couldn't go back to my room just yet. All it held was my bed, my books, my aging laptop. Too-yellow lights, fourth-hand furniture, chipped paint.

Instead, I let my bag slip from my shoulder to the grass, and then I settled down to join it, tail flopped limply behind me. I drew my knees up to my chest and crossed my arms over them, resting my chin atop my forearms.

My head was too full. Too full of words and feelings that language failed to express. Lines from the epistles I'd been studying somehow wound up tangled with an awkwardly-shaped despair, a despair founded in the fact that, although I continued to excel in my studies, remained at the top of my classes, I still felt as though I was failing.

If you still dwell within my heart, I asked. *Where are these feelings coming from? What is this disillusionment pointing to?*

God spoke to me, then.

As ever, His voice was not in words, but woven into the world around me. A breeze came up from Stump lake, bearing with it the scent of water, of rotting vegetation, and overlaid atop it, a sweetness I could not place. It was floral, yes, but also fruity, so sweet as to make my mouth water.

I bristled my whiskers, and breathed in deeply, my eyes scanning trees lit by the occasional yellow sulfur lamp, stark battlements against the night sky. God spoke to me in the way my eyes perceived the night to fade from a blue-tinged gray at the tree-line up to the star-stained black above me. He spoke in the feeling of the short blades of grass poking up through the bristly fur of my tail, and He spoke in the citrus tang of a confession forming in my mouth.

"I don't want to be here."

30

It would be incorrect to say that the hike I took yesterday in some way "solved" the anxiety that I felt after the concert. There were, as

I constantly tell myself, explain and explain and explain, no words from God. How would there be? How would it be the case that He would step in and say, "No, Dee, don't worry"?

I am trying not to get down on myself enough to lose all hope. I want to say, "This is so unimportant that I really need to just give up on the prospect." I want to recognize the futility in striving for a relationship. I want to buy into the egodystonia. I want to find some way to turn off that part of my mind that craves Kay, that dreams about the feeling of her cheek against mine and perseverates about holding her hand. How childish! How immature! How utterly beneath me that I struggle so hard with this!

But whatever.

I can't just turn all of those things off, but I *can* go ahead and admit that this isn't going anywhere. I can recognize that she wouldn't be a good romantic partner for me and I wouldn't be for her, and, even if the feelings don't go away, drop any hope of pursuing them. We Catholics are so good at repression, are we not?

There's nothing to be had but friendship, and I can aim for that, at least.

Today, Kay took me to a used bookstore near campus, and we spent a good hour and a half there, digging through the shelves. She sold me almost instantly on the place with the explanation that this was the type of place that would eagerly buy up all of the weird and obscure books that students pick up in their studies. Not just textbooks, though they certain took some of those when the university bookstore would not buy them back, but supplementary materials and personal hyperfixation-induced deep-dive book purchases.

Kay spent most of that time prowling through the music section, and me digging among shelves of exegeses and commentaries[29]. Occasionally, we would head back to the other to show them something of particular interest that we had found. At one point, she brought me a book on harmony written by some composer and laughingly read aloud a short section from the beginning, a scathing indictment of music critics, and we agreed that he must have, at some point, had a concert ripped to shreds in the papers. I brought her a whole stack of apologetics by C. S. Lewis and we reminisced over reading *The Chronicles of Narnia* as kits.

I do not think I could come up with a more ideal bookstore, I have to say. It was almost the platonic ideal of a used bookstore. Friends always talk about the scent of books being intoxicating, and while I've always been somewhat mixed on it[30], the scent of bookstores themselves are something that I am immensely fond of. It's not just the smell of the books that does it for me, but the shelves, the people, the lingering scent of those who might have handled the books before me. This book makes my whiskers bristle at the lingering scent of anxiety, that one was clearly loved and brought comfort. Whiskers bristle and I lose myself in the past of the place. There is something meta about the whole experience: books and also readers of those books.

I left after spending a surprisingly small amount of money on a surprisingly large number of books. The problem of fitting them all into my luggage for the trip home is a problem for future Dee.

Following the bookstore, we walked a block to an Ethiopian restaurant. I had never tried such cuisine before and while it was

---

[29] And bibles. Countless bibles.

[30] It can get rather close to the scent of mildew, which makes me quite uncomfortable. Scent is complicated.

not unpleasant, I am still trying to puzzle out the tastes.

The rest of the day was spent lounging at Kay's place, reading. She parked herself in her computer chair so that she could listen to her scores and insisted that I just use her bed — there being no other place to sit — so I propped myself up against the wall with her pillows and poked through my haul.[31] It wasn't the most comfortable of seats, and I had to dedicate a small portion of my mind at all times to ignoring the scent of Kay clinging to the sheets and pillowcases, but it was enjoyable arranging and rearranging the stack in what order might be best to read them in.

Kay, for her part was doing much the same, and whenever I would look over, she would be chewing on her cheek or a claw. She kept tapping out rhythms on the page of whatever page of a score she was looking at, humming arpeggios, and at least once I caught her nodding and tapping her tail about behind her, and when she looked up and saw me, she smiled bashfully and mumbled an apology.

It was a pleasant afternoon, all told, and we followed it up with a simple dinner of chicken that she cooked on her ancient stove and more shared videos, as has long been our habit.

Now I am back in the room that I'm staying in, surrounded by the non-scent of scent-block hiding whoever had stayed there before me, layered over with a thin darkness of my own scent.

I am embarrassed to admit that the change of scentscape has

---

[31] I picked up a few commentaries, a few that were more along the lines of pop-theology and a few that were quite dense and reminded me strongly of my time at St. John's to the point where I could almost smell the study room I spent so many hours in, the scratched desk and rickety chair. I also acquired books on psychology that I'd heard about from colleagues and had been meaning to read. Of note were two books on shame and vulnerability. How appropriate.

left me a little jarred today, in particular due to the fact that it had clearly been a few days since she had washed her sheets, and there was an unmistakable undertone of what I take to be sexuality clinging to those sheets. I do not doubt that she gets as aroused as any other healthy coyote of her age might, and I imagine that she is no stranger to masturbation. This is in no way surprising and yet I was in a continual state of tense wariness and low-level arousal of my own that I desperately hoped she could not smell in turn.

That, above all things is what I found myself needing to tune out. I buried my nose in book after book, and while that meant more than a mere whiff of mildew, it was less distracting by far.

I am trying to square my feelings about this. I am not immune to attraction, but the levels to which this complicates my feelings is uncomfortable. Here I am trying to convince myself to drop my attraction to her and my limbic system works against me.

I am not ashamed to admit that physiological response, but I am ashamed that I was unable to keep myself from acting on it — it seemed necessary if I was to sleep in any level of comfort. I shall have a confession in my future, but then, I knew that already.

31

All these little memories, all of them are coming back to me, and I'm not sure why. Nothing about this visit in particular ought to dredge them up, right? I mean, Kay and I have only talked passingly about faith, and sure, I didn't attend mass this weekend and am missing it, but there is little to suggest that this have anything to do with the flood of the small things from the past. Is it the lingering sensation of discernment?

Or perhaps it's talking with God. Perhaps it's less Kay than it is the way in which I'm approaching this whole situation. She herself is not bringing these out in me, but I am recapitulating so many of the same patterns I went through during my discernment.

I wrote before about certain embarrassing things sticking in the mind of the one embarrassed. We Catholics, we are so good at that. We're so good at picking the embarrassing things and hanging them up on the wall, admiring them, and then inviting others to share in the embarrassment with us. Our confessors are the witnesses to our shame. All we can hope is that they provide relief, and yet perhaps that is why so many confessions stick within the mind.

"Bless me, Father, for I have sinned. It has been one week since my last confession, and I accuse myself...I accuse..."

Other than the soft sounds of breathing and the barest hint of vulpine beneath the scent-block, nothing made its way from the other side of the screen, familiar even so many years after the fact, even long after I left Saint John's

"I accuse myself of the sin of doubt."

"You know that doubt is not a sin, my child."

"I guess, but my doubt is in my vocation."

"I see. Do you doubt in God?"

"No, no. Just...I find myself doubting, uh...I find myself doubting my upcoming role in the Church."

"What about the Church do you doubt, if your faith is solid?"

"I can't put my finger on it."

There was a quiet sigh from the other side of the screen.

"I guess my sin is that I am doubting my ability to actually serve God like I'm supposed to."

"What makes you think that?"

I shrugged helplessly. "I don't do well in front of crowds. No matter how much I try to fix that, I just can't. I doubt that I will ever be able to."

"I see."

It was my turn to wait in silence. Eventually, I bowed my head and said, "That is all, Father. For these and all of my sins, I ask forgiveness from God, and penance and absolution from you."

There was a pause, and then, "Alright, I will ask you to say three Our Fathers for doubting the path that God has laid out for you. It could be that you are still discovering this path, but doubt will only hinder you from carrying out His works. However, my son–" The priest rushed to forestall any response, and I remember hearing a smile creeping into his voice. "Outside of your penance, I would also like you to talk to your advisor. As your confessor, I can only offer you spiritual guidance."

I splayed my ears, chagrined, and bowed my head. "Thank you, Father."

With the final *go in peace* still ringing in my ears, with the tips of my fingers still humming from crossing myself, with the hot flush of embarrassment still pulling at my cheeks, I stepped from the confessional and blinked in the sudden light and space. I took two quick, grounding breaths, and then walked from the chapel.

I do not want to be here. The thought had become a mantra.

Outside, I walked slowly to one of the concrete blocks that served as benches and sat, resting my face in my paws. If I could not see the stars, if I had only concrete and paving stones before me, then if I wanted to pray, I had to block out my sight. It was all too much. I would find myself tracing the paving stones or the catenary arc of the contemporary entrance to St. Francis Abbey if I left them open.

> *Out of the depths I cry to you, O Lord. Lord, hear my voice! Let yours ears be attentive to the voice of my supplications...*

I was not ready yet. Not ready for my penitential *pater noster*. Not ready to go see my advisor. I didn't feel ready for anything.

Most of all, I realized I was not ready to admit to myself that not wanting to be here implied the possible solution of leaving, of *not* being here. I wasn't ready.

> *...If you, O Lord, should mark iniquities, Lord, who could stand? But there is forgiveness with you so that you may be revered...*

I didn't even feel ready for this prayer, for this call out to God. What iniquities faced me? I was privileged to be able to attend such a school as this. I was loved by God and the church and loved them in turn. I was lucky to have been born with a mind so expansive, a body so healthy.

Perhaps the iniquities were within. Perhaps it was something about myself, within myself, a core aspect of myself. Perhaps the privilege was undeserved. Just a coyote, right? Just a farmer, right? And yet here I was, languishing at a renowned seminary.

> *...I wait for the Lord, my soul waits, and in His word I hope; my soul waits for the Lord more than those who watch the morning, more than those who watch the morning.*

And so I waited.

I wished it were night. I wished I could sit in the quad and look up at the stars, or down at the grass and try to differentiate the shades of green, there in the dark where color eluded me, to find in that liminal state some sensation of the Lord.

At least I could get up from where I was and away from this edifice of concrete and glass. It was, I had been promised, beautiful in its own way. But behind the Abbey, toward the lake, a small path wound through the woods, and there, between the trees and beside the water, stood the statue of St. Kateri Tekakwitha, the only canonized coyote I'd ever come across, and the saint most venerated by my father back home.

...O Israel, hope in the Lord! For with the Lord there is steadfast love, and with him is great power to redeem...

I was not the farmer my family was, had few enough ties to her patronage of ecology and environmentalism, but in her I saw at least a face like my own. In her, I saw something of a people I could belong to, though she was from far to the east of my home in Idaho.

Home.

Home was back in Sawtooth, for Saint John's would never truly be my home, and that in itself was telling.

...It is He who will redeem Israel from all its iniquities.

Redeem Israel.

Israel, who struggled with God.

I envied, as I often did, the comment I had heard of the Jewish tradition about that eternal argument about who God was, what He meant, in which God was an active participant. Perhaps here, I could wrestle with Him. Tumble with my faith. Get all scuffed up.

But Catholicism only offered him so much leeway, and this school even less.

"I don't want to be here," I confessed to the statue. I remember that. I remember the kindness in the stone, in her smile. I confessed, then sighed, sat at her feet, and began my penance.

It had been a long trip home, from Saint John's back to Sawtooth.

I was hardly run out of the campus the moment of my decision. I was given the remainder of the month to wrap up my affairs and attend to the task of packing my meager belongings in order to move out of my room and bus back to Idaho, to Sawtooth. To home.

It was more than enough. My stuff was packed into two file boxes within an hour. After all, all of the furniture in the room belonged to the school. What had I besides clothes and books? Clothes, books, and my rosary.

I carried it with me always, then, my fingers marching through the decades of beads as words tumbled through my mind, spilled from my mouth without a sound. Over the next two weeks, I prayed the rosary dozens of times. Hundreds of *Hail Marys* and *Our Fathers*.

I knew not what drew me to begin this litany of prayer. I strive to pray the rosary every day, as a rule, but then, I needed that reassurance of faith. I needed some outward sign — whether to myself or to those around me I wasn't sure — that this decision was one of vocations, not of faith.

With my possessions packed away, I had little to do beyond pray and spend as much time in the library as I could before it would no longer be available to me.

"Technically," Borenson had confided when providing me instructions for those last few weeks. "You shouldn't have access to anything but the refectory, the chapel, and your room for the remainder of your time on campus, but I don't think anyone will begrudge you access to your beloved books."

The library and the woods, the quad, the lakes, the sky.

The Saint Bernard was waiting for me, sitting on the stone and cement bench by the statue of St. Kateri Tekakwitha. The dog had rested his elbows on his knees and clasped his hands, and was looking down between his feet through the opening this had created. Or, well, not looking. Father Borenson was not looking at anything. He had the absent expression of thought or prayer.

I had been making a round of all my favorite spots on this, my last day, and my final stop was here. A statue, a stone bench, a lake. Trees and heavy air.

I stood awkwardly by the statue, unsure of what to do with my advisor — my old advisor — present. This had always been a place of solitary engagement for me. Were it anyone else, I would have left and aimed to come back a little later. I still had an hour before I needed to head to the bus station.

"Afternoon, Mr. Kimana."

"Father. Sorry if I disturbed you. I can come back later."

The dog shook his head and leaned back against the bench, patting the spot next to him. "I was waiting for you, actually. I was hoping I'd catch you before you left."

After a moment's hesitation, I accepted the invitation and sat down, paws resting in my lap. Conversing sitting side by side like this was a mixed blessing. I didn't feel obligated to maintain eye contact, which was always a relief, but I was also left with the disconcerting feeling that there was a place I *ought* to be looking, that it ought to be at what whoever I was speaking with was looking at.

No wonder I wasn't cut out for this.

Borenson was the first to break the silence. "Dee, do you know what discernment is?"

"I'm assuming you mean in regards to figuring out one's calling?"

"Mmhm. Discerning whether you're heading toward married life, ministry, hermitage, whatever." He shook his head and laughed. "Sorry, this is one of those last-day conversations, and it's kind of difficult."

I nodded numbly. This was already wildly outside of my normal interactions with Borenson. Less academic, more informal, emotional.

"We don't really tell our students because we want you to come in feeling devoted, but there's a whole set of guidelines already in place behind the scenes to deal with this. Has been for centuries, really. Used to be, you'd be whisked away before you had the chance to even say goodbye. We'd box up your stuff and send it to you. It was a different church back then.

"Now, we see it more like a process. Discernment is something that takes place over time. You're in your twenties, you're not going to have it all figured out, much as you might sometimes imagine."

I frowned. *St. Kateri Tekakwitha,* I prayed silently.

Favored child and Lily of the Mohawks, I come to seek your intercession in my present need. I don't know what to do...

"It's a little clumsy, but the analogy I always use is to think of these first few semesters of your degree like dating. You and the church — the church as an institution, not just a faith — like each other, and want to maybe get closer, but you're going to try things on for size for a bit. See how it works out."

Outwardly, I nodded. "That makes sense. It's not a divorce, just a break-up before it gets serious."

Inwardly, I was doing my best to let go. Let go of this place. Let go of my study. Let go of the idea that I had built up over so long a time of what life would be like.

I admire the virtues which adorned your soul: love of God and neighbor, humility, obedience, patience, purity and the spirit of sacrifice. Help me to imitate your example in my state of life.

"Right," the Saint Bernard nodded. "Just turns out you and the Church get along better as friends than in...well, the metaphor breaks down somewhat here, but you can see how ordination is rather like marriage."

I smiled weakly. "Yeah."

"All this is to say that I think you're doing the right thing, because no one wants a bitter priest. Some folks might think ill of you, but don't worry about them. You've got your path ahead of you still, and God needs saints more than He needs priests."

Through the goodness and mercy of God, Who has blessed you with so many graces which led you to the true faith and to a high degree of holiness, pray to God for me and help me.

I stared at the statue of the coyote. I knew that if I were to try and look at Father Borenson, to engage with this conversation any more directly, I would not be able to keep from crying.

"I'll leave you be, Dee, but before I do, I'm curious. What will you do after this?"

I worked on mastering the lump of emotion swelling in my chest before replying. "I'm going to go home, stay with my parents. Work on the farm for a bit. Then, um…" I swallowed drily in an attempt to sound less hoarse. "Then I think I'm going to transfer to University of Idaho. I've been looking at maybe social work."

Borenson perked up, his tail thumping against the concrete and stone of the bench. "A therapist, hmm?"

"Yeah. I really do want to do good in the world, I just…well, perhaps a different kind." I let my shoulders slump. "I can't…I can't lead a congregation, but maybe I can manage something one-on-one."

"Of course," the dog laughed. "I can certainly see you excelling at that."

I smiled gratefully.

Standing up and brushing off his slacks, Borenson offered me his paw. It dwarfed mine, surrounding it in soft pads and softer fur. It made me feel uncouth, coarse, common.

"Mr. Kimana, it's been a pleasure."

I stood as well and turned the helping paw into a shake. "Thank you, Father."

"I wish you the best of luck. You're always welcome to come visit." The dog relinquished his grip, turned to the statue, crossed himself, and walked back toward campus.

Alone again, I turned from the statue and stared out over the lake. One final time, I asked if I was doing the right thing, and one final time, God spoke to me in the gentle lapping of the water at the shore, in the quiet hum of a bee in flight, in the sweet taste of surety in my mouth.

I stretched, crossed myself before the statue of St. Kateri Tekakwitha, brushed my fingertips over her stone paws, and then began to walk back through the campus.

It was a long trip home.

32

Relatively little happened for the rest of our visit, but we did rather front-load our plans. There was the movie, the concert, then I did my hike, and after that, we spent the rest of the visit just kind of...hanging out.

We spent a lot of time reading together. Reading and listening to music. Kay spent a morning putting together a playlist of songs that she knew that we both liked, and we listened our way through that as each of us skimmed through our books — at least, I skimmed through mine. Kay didn't seem keen on reading through her newly-purchased scores while other music was playing, and I certainly don't begrudge her that. Instead, she raced through a few novels that she had pulled from her bedside table.

We talked, too, of course. Once we had fallen back into the rhythm of being around each other, and once that initial bump of the concert was over, we opened up more. I spent a good amount of time talking to her about a lot of my memories surrounding Saint John's, and she talked about growing up with parents that were largely perplexed by her and who largely perplexed her in turn.

She freely admitted that she did not have the slightest clue about where I was coming from when it came to the topic of my discernment, and that to an extent, she had no desire to learn, but that she was still pleased to hear me talk through it, just as I promised her that I was pleased to listen to her talk through her music.

I mostly managed to keep my yap shut when she talked about her parents and youth. Something about growing up autistic with autistic parents was outside of my realm of experience, and the desire to dig deeper into that was strong, but she seemed to need to speak her thoughts out loud more than she needed the process of sharing.

It made sense to me, too. After all, that's what I've been doing to a greater or lesser extent with this journaling experiment, and I am certainly getting plenty out of simply stating aloud my memories of and thoughts on discernment.

Leaving her behind was sad, of course. I wished that I could spend more time with her even just doing nothing, just being normal together, despite also being glad that I was heading home. Sad, yes, but not in the way that I expected, I think.

I will miss her, that goes without saying, and I wish that I had more time to be close to her, but I was was also distraught due to the mess that my emotions were left in after we said goodbye.

Nothing changed between us.

Nothing changed, and I am struggling with the competing thoughts of:

- Of *course* nothing changed. We were friends going into this, we were friends during the visit, and we are friends now that it's over; and
- I wish that I had had the courage to tell her, such that things might have had the possibility of changing.

I am a coward.

We have such a solid basis for our friendship. We share hobbies, our communication styles line up almost perfectly, and we are comfortable in our silences together. We even share tastes in food[32], for heaven's sake.

But I'm a coward. I wanted this to be an incredibly meaningful and emotionally fulfilling visit. I wanted to have long, heartfelt conversations about how I felt and I wanted to understand her better than I did before. I wanted to see if there was the possibility for something more.

I am a coward and I am greedy and I am, I'm realizing, a narcissist, and that is why I'm distraught.

I will miss her.

I will miss her scent, even though it still clings to me after that last hug at the bus stop.

I will miss her voice, though I promised to call her once I made it back to my place in one piece.

I will miss her wit and her sarcasm and her intellect, though we will doubtless continue to talk every day.

I'm sad to be leaving her behind, but beyond that, I am sad to see what I have become, what limerence has made me. I am sad that I have been split in half. I am sad that I am less of an entire being when I think of her, and I am sad that I can't help but think of her. I am sad that some part of me has decided that she is just a limerent object rather than a friend, that I am the subject, and that even if the feelings I have for her *were* real — for now I'm sure that they aren't — I am too much of a coward to actually do anything about it.

Limerence, I have read, fades when feelings are either reciprocated or rebuffed, and yet neither happened, so I am back to hoping

---

[32] So long as it isn't lent, of course. She requires meat with every meal, she joked at one point, and I laughed, though I am not sure how much innuendo was behind that comment. Innuendo! Look at you, Dee, all grown up, thinking about innuendo.

against hope that they simply fade with time. I don't want them, these feelings. I don't want to feel this way. I don't want to be crying while writing about a girl on a steno pad in an uncomfortable bus seat.

33

I miss my friend.

I miss Kay, yes. I miss being with her, but I miss her as a friend. I miss having her be someone I can turn to. I miss having her in my life with none of these dramatic feelings pinned to her, feelings I have no way of removing.

I'm tired and I'm anxious and I'm tired of being anxious.

I miss my friend.

34

When I look back at some of the entries from during and immediately after my trip, they all sound so bleak. They make it sound like I did not enjoy it, when I clearly did. I focus a lot on my time spent away from Kay. I focus a lot on memories. I focus a lot on that yearning tugging at my chest whenever I was around her.

And honestly, I don't think that's fair to what actually happened. I *did* enjoy my time around her. I enjoyed it immensely. When we were walking, when we were just ceaselessly rambling at each other about the things we find fascinating, when we went out to lunch, it was all this really delightful mix of nostalgia and connection that went beyond just the desire for anything more. I said in a previous entry that, if limerence is an unwanted emotional attraction, maybe all I really want to do with/for Kay is be the best friend to her that I possibly can. I want to make her happy, and that, in turn, will make me happy as well.

I put that to work when I was with her. We went out to coffee several times at that café near my rented room, and spent a while just talking. We even went for a hike together and, though it lacked the spiritual savor of my other hike in the Reserve, it was still a meaningful experience for me.

And yet, I didn't write about those times, or touched on them only briefly.

I look back through my entries from the visit and wonder why it is that I wrote only about yearning, when I was writing about Kay. I apparently had a hard time putting down the quotidian, all the just plain *hanging out* that we did together, and instead focused on the burning inside me that craved more than that. It was a form of catastrophizing.

That's not fair to her, that's not fair to me, and that's not fair to the truth of what it is that I think I would actually get out of a relationship with her.

It was that last part that got me me thinking and reading, and I came across an idea that the sheer intensity of limerence had obscured, which is that, above all else, one's partner should be one's best friend, someone who you know will be there with you, share your moments with you. Someone you love and who loves you back, of course, but beyond that, someone who is a part of your life that goes beyond just base-level friendship and up into best friends territory, and beyond.

I think that, right now, I would call Kay my best friend. Unsurprising, of course, given how few friends I have outside of my friendship with her. I am cordial with folks from work and have gotten lunch with several, and there are quite a few folks from church that I have spent time with outside of that context, but, while I care about them, I don't care about them to nearly the same extent that I care about Kay.

I read back through all of those entries and, while I don't wish to put words into her mouth, I sense in her many of the same thoughts. She talked about how few people she keeps up with from Sawtooth, and she mentions having picked up the habit of apologizing to others for talking in the same, excited way that she talks with me, and in that, I see best-friendship.

And if I put those together, if I think of it this way and add that romantic devotion to what is otherwise a friendly devotion, if I turn *philia* into *eros*, then is that not a deepening of that friendship? Is that not moving forward? Is that not progress?

I sound so close to giving up, in those entries. I sound like someone who is struggling with their feelings rather than the mechanics of the relationship (though I do note that Kay brings up the mechanical point of our differences in approach to religion, to put it charitably).

I am not one to unconditionally say that all progress is good, but much of it is, and honestly, at this point, I struggle to see the ways in which progressing our relationship would be a negative.

So, enough equivocation. I think it's time to tell her. To ask her. To, if nothing else, find out where we stand and see what futures lay ahead of us.

35

Over the last few days, I have been sending Kay a few emails. I am ashamed to admit that this is an intentional aspect of some grander plan. One could say that it is to get her re-accustomed to getting emails from me, though this is a somewhat less than charitable way of looking at it.

In reality, it is a way for me to psych myself up for sending what I hope to be the email wherein I discuss my feelings for her. It's less that she needs some sort of preparation for simply receiving an email, and more that I need to get myself ready to *actually* click the button that sends it.

I am clearly struggling with this process if I am feeling the need to not only psych myself up to email someone but also journal about the process of psyching myself up.

I am, as always, a coward. That I even need to do this over email is proof enough of that.

Anyway, here is what I am thinking that I will send her tomorrow — it is getting late today and I want to be awake for the whole process.

Kay

If you had told me, over the years that we have known each other, that I would be writing to you like this, I wouldn't have believed you. It's a strange enough act on its own, sending you an email, but to do so like this, to send something like this, is so strange as to border on the ludicrous.

We've known each other for a good, what, five years now? And have been friends for a good chunk of that time. For some reason, we just kind of click when we really get going talking to each other, sharing whatever thing we're interested in at the time. We share a lot of the same idiosyncrasies, verbal habits, and even coping mechanisms.

Lately, I have noticed something of a change in myself. I've always enjoyed your company, of course, but I have noticed that my feelings of friendship are starting to take on a romantic bent.

I'm sure that I could go on, as you know I am prone to doing, but that would only muddy the point. Needless to say, I like you Kay, and am starting to admit to myself that I am liking you more as time goes by. And though I've been hesitant to put it in such words even to myself, I think I'm falling in love with you.

I don't know how to do this. I am a consummately awkward person by my own admission, and I've never had to admit that I've started to feel romantic toward someone before. Perhaps that's weird. Normal people, I suspect, have told several people that they're in love by the time that they're nearing thirty, but, well, it has just never been on my radar.

I feel compelled to say that you are under no obligation to return these feelings toward me. If you don't feel the same way, that's completely fine, and I hope that this will not negatively impact your view of me as a friend.

This is a feeling I've had toward you, but it need not be the *only* feeling I have.

But, on the chance that this is a mutual feeling between us, I would like to deepen our relationship beyond friendship. As stated, I have no idea how to do this, so I suppose I'm asking you out 😺

Again, no worries if not! I am simply happy to have you as my friend.

Best,

Dee

I have slaved over these words so long that I think I nearly have the letter memorized. It's silly, in a way, to put this much energy into something, but this entire process has been silly. It's been silly since I caught myself having dreams about her, and before even that, when I started this whole journal process.

But I am nothing if not deliberate, and this feels like the proper way to undertake a discernment, though I find that term most often in a religious context. I am digging deep into all of my thoughts, stripping away the extraneous ones, and then boiling the remainder down into an admission. An admission to myself, but also one that I can send to Kay.

I will think on it and pray on it for one more night before sending it, but honestly, of all of the decisions that I've made around this entire debacle, if it can be called that, this one feels the most freeing. It feels like me opening a little bit of space for myself.

It was all well and good for me to reduce my feelings to trying to be the best friend I could be for her[33], and one ought to keep in mind the selfless in one's life, but, well, one cannot be a truly good friend while withholding information. I cannot, at least. I can't be a good friend while continuing to tear myself up inside over this. I called myself a narcissist before in these pages, but, while perhaps some of my thoughts have been narcissistic, that is far to strong a word than required for simply striving for happiness.

I will think, I will pray, and then I will click "send".

36

As promised, I spent this morning thinking and praying on the letter, and in true Dee form, this involved getting a ride to a trail head up by the foothills and going for a walk.

My mind was too busy and unsettled to do much other than attempt to sort feelings into differently labeled and sized boxes. I ran through an internal checklist of all the things that had happened leading up to this decision, all the steps along the path of discernment. I ticked them off one by one as I filed them on various shelves, then went back through and erased all of the check marks and filed them on different shelves. It was exhausting, being unable to let go of a thought, like a cut on the inside of one's muzzle or a zit at the base of a whisker, something you can't help but poke and prod at ceaselessly in the hopes that maybe something will help.

Eventually, I simply got too tired to continue thinking like that. I was panting by now, the cool air of the foothills drawing heat from me and leaving my tongue dry and lolling. I realized that I had

---

[33] Something I aim to do for her regardless.

nearly jogged up the hill from the trail head, and had made it much further than I had intended while so preoccupied.

I considered heading back into town before it got too hot out, but instead, I found a rock off to the side of the trail that wasn't too dusty, and I sat down and looked out over what bits of Sawtooth I could see over the first real hill outside of town.

Scraps of buildings peeked out from the very south edge of downtown, then a mess of neighborhoods swept down south, affluence and age defined block by block. Out behind town toward the highway, the houses faded and warehouses sprouted in their place. Warehouses and workshops and anonymous, low-slung office buildings that doubtless housed call centers or data entry facilities or hyperspecific contractors.

And then beyond out into the scattered fields and grazing land. What green there was outside those fields was already fading into brown, and in the air the brown was echoed in a haze of dust or what smog dared collect above the town.

I wish that I could say that I talked with God then, like I have so many other times in this narrative. I wish I could tell you that he spoke to me in the slow dissolution of town into not-town. I wish I could say that I found beauty even in the right angles that nature so abhors, that even industry spoke to a sort of majesty all its own.

He didn't, though. He was silent. There was no surety to be had, there was no gentle nudges by that still, small voice this way or that.

I prayed the rosary instead, counting decades of *Hail Marys* and *Our Fathers* on beads worn smooth.

I couldn't even form a request, at that point. I couldn't talk to God, I couldn't come up with the words, all I could do was sit with myself and my thoughts and my rosary and a pulse racing at the tension of limerence within me, at the thought of all I could possibly have in my future.

I sat on that rock until I started to bake in the sun, then started to head back down the trail where I came. It had grown far too hot and I had to beg water off a better prepared mountain lion about halfway through my hike back to the trail head just to keep my lips and tongue wet as I puffed and panted.

At the lot, I called for another GetThere care to take me back home, back to my air-conditioned apartment where I could rehydrate and hem and haw until eventually, hopefully, maybe, I could finally hit send on that email and release this overwhelming tension within.

37

7:24 PM Dee
Been thinking.

7:26 PM Dee
We still talk a lot, and I really like that. For having only had a little bit of time together at UI, it's nice that we've been able to keep up with each other.

7:26 PM Kay
Yeah?

7:26 PM Kay
I mean, I like it too.

7:27 PM Kay
I only talk to you and like two classmates from that time, and one only because he's also up here in Boise.

7:27 PM Dee
Yeah.

7:28 PM Dee
So I don't know if this is weird or not. It's not something I've ever
done or

7:28 PM Kay
?

7:31 PM Dee
Not something I've ever done or really felt, but I think I really like
you.

7:31 PM Dee
Know I really like you.

7:31 PM Dee
And goodness knows I have no idea what to do about it.

7:31 PM Dee
It's taken me weeks to even get to the point where I could say that.

7:32 PM Kay
Huh...

7:33 PM Dee
???

7:34 PM Kay
I like you too, but I'm not sure if it's in the same way?

7:34 PM Kay
Assuming you mean romantically.

7:34 PM Dee
Yes.

7:35 PM Kay
Yeah, see.

7:35 PM Kay
I don't know.

7:35 PM Dee
I don't either, I guess.

7:37 PM Kay
I'm really not sure how to take this conversation haha

7:40 PM Kay
I hope that's not

7:40 PM Kay
I don't know

7:40 PM Kay
Painful?

7:45 PM Dee
Well.

7:45 PM Kay
Yeah, sorry...

7:45 PM Dee
No no, I mean

7:45 PM Dee
Well, it is, but that's not quite where I was going, hah.

7:46 PM Kay
Sorry. I'll let you type.

7:50 PM Dee
I don't really know what I wanted out of this conversation, to be honest. I wasn't even intending for it to be a conversation, at least right off the bat. I had a whole email written up that I was going to send you, to be perfectly nerdy about it.

7:54 PM Dee
Feelings like this aren't logical. At least, they don't feel logical So I think I just wanted to say that because I don't know what to do with all of them. They just boil up within me and I just sit there and feel weird and bad but also kind of good at the same time. I just started falling for you, and kept it to myself because it felt like such an imposition to admit that to you.

7:54 PM Dee
And I should add

7:55 PM Dee
The goal is specifically NOT to do that. It wasn't to try and rope you

into something you don't want to do, and I don't want to make it sound like I am trying to do so now.

7:55 PM Dee
Guilt you into it or whatever.

7:56 PM Dee
But I did want to talk about it and get it off my chest.

7:57 PM Dee
And I guess that's it.

7:57 PM Kay
Alright.

7:58 PM Kay
I mean, I don't think you could guilt the wings off a fly, Dee.

7:58 PM Kay
The whole Catholic thing is guilting yourself, right?

7:59 PM Dee
That's a bit of an uncharitable way to put it.

7:59 PM Kay
Sorry. You know I don't understand it.

7:59 PM Dee
Yeah.

8:00 PM Kay
And that's maybe part of it.

8:00 PM Dee
How so?

8:01 PM Kay
How would you feel being in a relationship with someone who doesn't believe the same stuff?

8:01 PM Kay
Doesn't believe ANY of it, I mean.

8:01 PM Kay
I'm not going to knock it or anything, but I'm not going to try it, either.

8:02 PM Kay
I'm sorry.

8:02 PM Dee
Hah.

8:02 PM Dee
Sorry, that came out weird?

8:06 PM Dee
Seriously, though, I really don't know. This whole thing, this whole crush or whatever it is, I don't know what the end goal of it is. It's limerence, it's something that's happening to me, and I don't know what to do about it. It's this enormous feeling and you're the limerent object, and I hate that my brain is doing it.

8:07 PM Dee
And at the same time, I really do like you, and that is something I am happy to accommodate even in the context of our friendship.

8:07 PM Dee
Because above all else, I'm simply happy to have you as my friend.

8:07 PM Kay
Same!

8:09 PM Dee
And even if a relationship isn't in our future, that's totally okay.

8:10 PM Kay
Thanks Dee <3

8:10 PM Kay
I don't know, it's weird.

8:11 PM Kay
I kind of suspected, now that I think back on it?

8:11 PM Kay
Not like you were being a weirdo.

8:11 PM Kay
Or any more than usual 😸

8:13 PM Kay
Just little things about how you acted when I was over. Nothing bad, just you had a certain distance about you, like you were being extra careful about something or guarding something. Like, every time you came over to my place and wound up sitting in my bed or something, you'd get all quiet.

8:13 PM Kay
I realize after the fact that that was probably super weird for you. Sorry about that.

8:14 PM Dee
Oh, are you saying I was more awkward than usual? Shock and surprise!

8:14 PM Kay
Haha

8:17 PM Dee
It was weird, but please don't put that on you. I just...yeah, I was fighting with my emotions at the time, and huddling on your bed where literally all I could smell was you and with you being the sole focus of my attention, it was...well.

8:18 PM Dee
Intense, I guess.

8:18 PM Kay
I bet.

8:18 PM Kay
Still, I'm sorry, Dee.

8:19 PM Kay
I won't say my 'no' is absolute and forever, I can't predict that, but it is a 'no' for now.

8:19 PM Dee
Thanks, Kay.

8:20 PM Dee
For being so open about it, I mean.

8:20 PM Dee

And honest, I guess.

8:21 PM Dee

Uh...and to continue being awkward for at least a moment longer, are you okay remaining friends?

8:21 PM Kay

Dee I swear to god

8:22 PM Kay

If you did anything to make me not want to be your friend any longer a) you would know it because I would kick your ass and b) I'd go fucking nuts because I wasn't kidding about you being just about the only friend I have that I can talk to.

8:22 PM Kay

We're friends, okay? If a friendship can't take a challenge, what even is it, then? :P

8:23 PM Dee

Haha. Well, good. I'm not keen on getting my ass kicked, and ditto. I'd rather have my nails pulled out that lose you as a friend.

8:23 PM Kay

Gross

8:23 PM Kay

8:25 PM Dee

It feels surprisingly good to get that out.

8:25 PM Kay

Even if it isn't the outcome you wanted?

8:26 PM Dee

It's weird.

8:27 PM Dee

I'm not sure what outcome it is that I really wanted.

8:29 PM Dee

I mean, not gonna lie, if we'd wound up going out or whatever, that would've been nice! But I don't think that was ACTUALLY my goal. I think I really just wanted to get it off my chest. I wanted to not be holding it in and feeling like an idiot any longer.

8:29 PM Kay
I bet!

8:30 PM Kay
How long has it been, anyway?

8:31 PM Kay
Shit. If you don't mind me asking, that is. I don't want to draw it out if this is just continuing to hurt you or anything 😿

8:32 PM Dee
No, it's okay! It's made me a weird, giggly mess for some reason because apparently I'm still twelve, admitting that I have a crush, but it's good to talk about.

8:32 PM Dee
Way better than an email would have been, yikes.

8:32 PM Dee
But it's been about six months? A bit longer?

8:33 PM Kay
Can I just say that you writing up a whole-ass email to tell me that you like me is the most Dee possible thing that I can think of?

8:33 PM Dee
Listen.

8:33 PM Dee
I set up an archetype for myself and have no choice but to live up to it.

8:33 PM Kay
Nerd

8:35 PM Kay
What was even in the email?

8:35 PM Dee
I still have it in drafts. Want me to just send it?

8:35 PM Kay
Sure

8:43 PM Kay
Oh Dee

8:43 PM Kay
This is incredibly sweet, jesus

8:43 PM Kay
fuck haha

8:43 PM Kay
got me all sniffly

8:44 PM Kay
You're still a total nerd

8:45 PM Kay
But whoever you wind up with is gonna be the luckiest gal out there

8:45 PM Kay
Man, I'm sorry

8:46 PM Dee
??

8:47 PM Kay
I feel like I'm teasing you by saying that 😺

8:47 PM Dee
I don't feel teased.

8:48 PM Dee
A bit...bashful, maybe?

8:48 PM Dee
And I'm not going to lie that hearing that makes me a little bit hopeful for the future, but I stand by what I said that I'm alright with your answer, and am happy to have you as a friend.

8:49 PM Kay
Uh

8:49 PM Kay
Yeah, I don't know

8:49 PM Kay

Let's talk about it in the future sometime, then? Because yeah, like

8:50 PM Kay

Maybe we could make it work?

8:51 PM Kay

But just not right now

8:51 PM Kay

I can picture it in my mind, and you're cute and sweet and we have fun, but I guess I just can't say yes right now.

8:52 PM Dee

For the future, then.

8:52 PM Dee

For now, I'm gonna go order some food. Not to put an artificial stopper in this, but maybe we can just chill with a movie or something after?

8:53 PM Kay

Yeah, sounds good 😺 Sci-fi bullshit?

8:53 PM Dee

Oh, definitely sci-fi bullshit.

38

All of my work on emotional literacy is failing me now. It was largely failing me then, as well. I am doing my best to process the conversation that we had here, but I am in a state of, I suppose, numbness, and that numbness is taking up the same amount of space that the limerence did before. It is overwhelming in its nullity, and there is nothing, it seems, that I can do to shake it. I cannot transmute it into something more positive.

But that said, the nullity is not negative. It is not a lack of any necessity. It is a lack, instead, of the too-full feeling of limerence that had once taken up a full half of my entire being.

That space, I imagine, will contract. I will slowly retract that distension back into myself. Not the self I used to be, but something new and changed, for after so long of having that bloat, a permanent mark has been left. I am changed. I am different.

Better? I hope so, but it is yet to be seen.

For the point of my subconscious strain has faded, and only the habit of doing so remains. Where before I would dream of getting the chance to hold Kay's hand or to lay in bed next to her or, and let's not mince words here as this is what journals are for, make love, I now dream about what that life would have looked like in greater clarity. Where before I would construct a counterfactual universe in which we lived a perfect life, in which her fur was as soft as it was in my dreams, I now construct counterfactual universes in which we got together and it was specifically *not* perfect, and I run down a list of all of the things that might have hindered perfection. Religion, sure, but what about that envy I felt at the concert? Was that a one-time thing? Would that have carried over? Would I be a possessive partner, or would that have relaxed? And so I imagine both.

I imagine us a few years down the line, sharing an apartment. I imagine which of us would have to move. Would I move my practice to Boise? Would she be content, as a musician, to live out here in Sawtooth? We have a good enough music program at the university that she got her bachelors out here, but that presupposes the fact that she might want to teach. Would we even stay in Idaho?

And how would us living together look, anyway? I have my little one-bedroom apartment that suits me in particular due to its solitude. It faces a ruddy creek that has been gussied up into something grander through landscaping and a meandering path. I like my solitude, but living together means having someone constantly in your space. Where would I get that solitude?

I have my apartment set up with a combination library/den/home office and my bedroom, while Kay has her computer in her bedroom which is also her living room which is also, for the most part, her kitchen. Where would she put her computer, and where would I put mine? Would we share a library? I imagine so; in my brighter imaginings, I picture how we might have looked, sitting on a couch by our combined bookshelves, each reading our own thing.

But the problem remains. We would have to get a two-bedroom apartment, at the very least, so that we could have separate office spaces, separate areas of privacy. An office and a shared bedroom? Do we split the office with some kind of divider? Do I keep my office in the living room?

And still, I picture it working. I picture us sharing a bed. I picture us parceling out chores. I picture us waiting for the other to finish using the bathroom and getting a little disgusted by lingering scents. I picture us getting tired of simple pasta with chicken or whatever, and deciding to learn how to cook something better because eating out is getting expensive.

And sure, I picture the sex. I have no idea whether Kay is a virgin, and don't particularly care, I think, but I am, and instead of fantasizing about perfect lovemaking, I picture us struggling to get our moods aligned, and I picture the process of at least me learning how to be intimate, and potentially the both of us.

A wedding? Would that be in our future? And if so, what does that look like? Do we have a long and occasionally heated process of discernment to decide whether or not she is okay with a Catholic wedding?

And oh yes, the church. Do we find our own unique way to agree to disagree? I have little enough iconography in my place, but I do have my mother's crucifix and my father's painting of Saint Kateri Tekakwitha on my walls, and I would not be comfortable removing either. I pray the rosary regularly. I attend mass every weekend, if possible. These are the facts of my life, and until confronted with these imaginings, I had not realized that they are all visible. Kay would be confronted with all of them on a daily basis.

And I would be confronted with her atheism. On the surface, I can see that being acceptable to me, and none of my immediate family is alive to question whether or not it is appropriate for me to marry outside the church, so I do not have to rely on approval.

I can see it being acceptable, except for the fact that a core aspect of my life is missing from hers. Me, Dee, the one who was on track to be Father Kimana. Visible or not, that is a divide that can only be bridged and never filled.

Oh, and should we have children, would they be raised Catholic? Would they be baptized? Would they attend mass and their mother not?

I can see it being acceptable, but I can also see it being an awful lot of work for the both of us.

Where are the compromises? Where are the fights? Where are we twenty, thirty, forty years down the line? Do we make it twenty, thirty, forty years? Are we so fit for each other that we can manage that?

Before, when limerence filled me to overflowing, I imagined in dreamy yeses and delicate physicality. Now that that has faded and left something else in its place, I imagine in questions. I imagine in what-ifs and is-it-actuallys.

In the end, though, I hope that this is better. More, I *believe* that it is better, this numbness that has taken its place. I believe it must be, because if there is one sensation that I can liken to this numbness, these imaginings, these feelings and emotions, it is healing.

Trite? Sure, but limerence was an unwieldy mass that laid claim to me, and, even at its best, I was opposed to that claim. I am healing from the wounds that it left when it dug its claws into me, when it was removed and left that hole where once it was.

I am free of it, I am healing, and all these imaginings and suppositions boil down to me desiring only that, should we wind up deciding some day down the line to get together, that we come across that jointly, consensually, honestly, syntonically, uninfluenced by that wildness of the heart, as past-Dee put it.

39

I closed my steno pad after the most recent entry, fully intending that that would be the last entry that I would write. The discernment, after all, was complete, even if only for a little while, and I no longer needed to puzzle it out on paper.

"That's bullshit and you know it," Jeremy laughed when I told him this fact.

I felt my ears redden. "You think I'll keep writing about it?"

"Of course I do, Dee. It's just how you work. I think you reached a milestone with this, and I'm honestly proud of you. You were always courageous, you know. You can think of it like a hill, you had to push and push and push, and you kept doing so even if you didn't really know you were. Then you hit the tipping point at the top of the hill and that courage came through and did its job."

I nodded and mumbled a thanks.

"So, yes, you reached a milestone, but the work isn't over, I bet. Are you ready to just drop back into your old friendship with Kay?"

After a moment's thought, I shook my head. "No. It's changed things plenty. The last few days feel like a renegotiation of boundaries. It feels like we're both being really careful around the other."

"Right," he said. "I imagine you'll have to learn how to be friends again, and that that friendship will look different."

"You think I should keep journaling on it, then?"

"I don't think you have a choice, bud," he laughed. "The stuff you sent me was you doing your best to process all of this, and I could see the work taking place. You just admitted the work will continue, so, yeah, keep it up. And anyway, you talk about your advisor saying that he would have been concerned if you *were* losing your faith, and Kay says that you writing her an email to tell her how you feel is the most you thing ever. I think you're basically stuck journaling."

It was my turn to laugh. "Right, right, okay. I'll keep it up, then."

"And hey, you can pull a lot of your thoughts on discernment and such out into a book or hell, clean these up and turn them into a memoir. It's not like this stuff is useful to only you."

That's been lingering with me, but I remain unsure. I could, yes, and maybe it would provide some sort of entertainment, but that would mean going through and editing everything up[34]. Even just the process of transferring notes from paper to computer so that I could email them to Jeremy had been rough enough, being con-

---

[34] I already felt compelled to add all of these footnotes, after all

fronted by that Dee of a few months back, struggling with the most basic language of actually liking someone.

I do agree with the first point that Jeremy made, though. I really ought to keep journaling. It's good for me, and I don't think I could ever really stop, after going through this.

So, yes. The work continues.

Kay broached the subject of stopping by UI Sawtooth for a concert some day and spending a bit of time together. The doors to friendship remain open, and I don't imagine that it will be *intolerably* awkward, but it will still present challenges. Would hugging be too awkward? Should we spend the whole trip together much like we did the last one?

As the next step of my *spiritual* discernment, I have reached out to the parish priest about offering free mental health counseling to less fortunate members of the congregation or those who stop by the mission the church runs in town and he is going to set up a meeting with the bishop of the diocese to see if there's space for such in a church-sanctioned context. I think that I would be happy enough to volunteer such on my own. It's not the spiritual counseling that I had once planned on after my undergrad, but it is something far more in my area of expertise and comfort zone.

All these things are part of the work, though. Work is part of life, and life goes on. I still see my clients. I still watch videos and talk about my days with Kay. I still go to mass. I still think about the past year when I write. I still get rides out to the edge of Sawtooth or over to a trail head and walk until my feet ache and I am gasping in the pine-scented, dusty air.

And still I talk with God.

Gigs

Well, shit.

Winter trudged heavily through the piles of dead leaves lining the gutter, the lynx's broad paws crunching through them. There was a sidewalk, but this wasn't a mood for sidewalks. This wasn't a mood for keeping clean, staying out of the way. This was a proper sulk.

She pulled her phone out for the umpteenth time and thumbed at the screen, tapping out yet another message to Katrin that she wouldn't send. Deleted message. Put phone away.

A low growl started in her chest, rose, crescendoed, and she let out a brief yell. No words, just a vent of frustration. Birds startled from the tree beside her.

It didn't help.

"Making a damn fool of yourself," she grumbled. "Twice over."

She hesitated on the corner of Linden and 18th, stopping mid-stride and staring down the street. She should turn. She should turn left and walk the next two blocks. She should head up the stairs. She should open the door, set her phone down, change out of her clothes — clothes she'd now have to return to the market — clean up, start cooking.

She should tell Katrin what happened. She should look for a new job.

"Shit," she repeated, this time aloud, and kept walking straight. Five blocks to the plaza. She'd grab a coffee, sit on one of the benches. Watch the early afternoon crowds putter along the mall.

Or maybe she shouldn't grab a coffee she could no longer afford. Maybe she should be saving her money.

She kept walking.

She got her coffee.

She sat, and she watched.

Katrin and Winter stood still, heads bowed, both searching through their thoughts.

Winter couldn't guess at her wife's thoughts. The fox was always so inscrutable. Winter would sometimes watch her face while the vixen worked, the blank mask of pure white, punctuated with only the pitch-black nose, those darkest-brown eyes, and try to decide if the inscrutable part was the all-white fur or some sort of Scandinavian magic.

Today, she couldn't tell. Katrin's matte-white fur reflected light so well that there were no shadows left to reflect her emotions. And yet, there was still something foreign to those features. The almond-shaped eyes, the blunt muzzle, the ears almost hidden in thick fur.

Perhaps another Swede would be able to read that face, to say what Katrin was feeling, but not Winter. Not right now.

"And they didn't give any recourse?" The fox looked up to Winter. "Just *come pick up your last paycheck and drop off your shirts?*"

The lynx nodded. "Just that. Mr. Stevenson just said he couldn't keep both managers on board, and, well, Kayla's his daughter."

Katrin nodded and slid her paw across the counter top to twine her fingers with the lynx's. "I understand. I'm sorry, love."

"It's okay." Winter sighed and gave those fingers a squeeze in her own. Even with the flour still clinging clinging to her wife's fur, even with the coarseness of her pads, worn from so much kneading of dough, they seemed so delicate in her thick-furred mitts. "I'll start looking tomorrow."

"Okay. Let me know if you need any help, I'll do what I can."

The lynx nodded.

"It'll be okay, love. I promise." Her smile was tired.

Gone were the days of sitting up at the kitchen table, circling help-wanted ads in the newspaper. Hell, gone were the days of the newspaper.

Instead, Winter grew addicted to job posting boards, both local to her town and some that ran on a wider scale. Once she got her résumé all fixed up, she began flooding local stores with it, starting with all of the local grocers — as Stevenson's had been — and then broadening her search to related retail outlets.

And then unrelated.

Then non-retail positions.

She would work in shifts, spending an hour prowling through postings, then spending five minutes making sure her files were in order, then another two hours applying. The act of uploading a résumé to a site that promised to read all it could from it, then required her to fill in all that information again in form fields became rote, numbing.

There were a few calls back, but more often than not, silence. It was starting to feel futile. It was starting to feel like hollering into the void. She would click submit on yet another application, and it would just...go away. It would go nowhere.

Even an outright rejection would feel better.

She had set herself a week to exhaust all of the usual application channels. On the third or fourth day, she started driving around to stores and dropping off paper copies of her applications as well.

It was on one of those outings towards the end of her time-boxed week that she first noticed the ride share sticker in someone's window.

"Winter? For Malina?"

"Yep, that's me," the lynx replied cheerfully.

"Great!" The badger hauled a few sacks of groceries into the back seat and slid in after them. "Thanks so much for the ride. Car's in the shop and all."

"Oh, no worries." Winter waited for Malina to get herself buckled in before tapping at the GetThere app on her phone to set the satnav to direct her to the badger's destination. "Hopefully nothing expensive?"

Malina laughed. "Shouldn't be. One of those warranty things. A part recall or something. I'm out a car for a day or two, but at least I don't have to pay for it."

"No loaner, then? Do they even still do that?"

"I'm not sure, honestly. They might. But either way, I'm within walking distance from work, so I figured it wouldn't be that big of a deal." With a wry smile, she added, "I just wasn't counting on having to do a grocery run for work. Starts getting cold out, and we start mowing through milk."

Winter slid the car back into traffic — mercifully light today — and started down the road back toward 13th. "Fair enough. Where do you work, that you go through milk so fast?"

"A coffee shop. The Book and the Bean, on the plaza. There's a few shops within walking distance that sell dairy, but none of them sell the more exotic milks, so I have to head further out. Easy enough to walk there, but I'm not hauling all of this back."

"Oh, yeah! I know the one. My wife's restaurant, Middagsbord, is just down the block." She grinned. "I doubt those bags are light, though, yeah."

Malina laughed and shook her head. "Not at all."

There were a few moments of silence as Winter negotiated a left turn and the badger in the back seat thumbed through her phone.

"How about you?" came a distracted voice from the back. "Is this your full-time thing? Driving?"

Winter shook her head. "Not exactly. I just started this not too long ago. This and random gigs on Simpletask."

"What's that?"

"Just random things people want done but don't want to do themselves. I've done filing, transcription, cataloging...boring stuff, really."

Malina nodded. "Sounds like driving's the more interesting of the two."

"Wasn't really my first choice, but it's turning out to be way more fun than I thought it would be."

"Oh yeah? What about it do you like? Setting your own hours?"

"I try to work pretty standard hours, though for me that means working morning rush hour driving, doing some tasks, driving during lunch, more tasks, and then evening rush hour." Winter thought for a moment, then continued, "No, I think the thing I like about it is that it gets me a lot of the best things I liked about retail without the standing all day or dragging boxes around."

In the rear-view mirror, Malina grinned. "Yeah, that makes sense. Just the meeting people sort of thing?"

"Mmhm. Meeting people, being helpful. People are generally kinder here than they are in stores, too. Most folks are grateful for the rides, and those that aren't having a good day are usually pretty quiet. I don't get many people hollering at me."

Malina laughed. "Oh, I know that one. I used to work in finance, but got sick of it. I figured moving to where I saw people instead of numbers would be easier on the soul. I was mostly right."

"Mostly?"

"Yeah. A lot of people are grateful for coffee, but like you said, those who aren't tend to holler."

It was Winter's turn to laugh. "Yep, that's the type. I guess that's what I mean, though. I got good at the sort of happy retail mask that one puts on around them, but I haven't needed it here. Not as much, at least."

As expected, the drive was a short one. Once they made it to the loading zone at the end of the 13th Street Plaza, Winter helped Malina unload the bags of milk and other sundries from the back of her car.

"Thanks again, Winter," the badger said, loading herself up once again. "Stop in any time."

The lynx nodded and waved before hopping back in her car and turning off the hazard lights.

While the biggest benefit to this new form of employment was the free-form nature of it, that very benefit worked against it. It was up to Winter to schedule her day around the best times for driving, and the best times for working on projects on Simpletask.

However, when Sawtoothians needed rides was unsteady. Sure, there were times when rides were more likely: rush hour, some time over lunch, Thursday, Friday, and Saturday nights. She started keeping track of sporting events, concerts, and conferences.

Some days, Winter would be flooded with rides, and the lynx would dart all over town, picking up passengers of all stripes and driving them to some concert venue or the UI-Sawtooth campus stadium.

And some days, she would be stuck on her laptop at The Book and the Bean — Malina having convinced her to become a regular — waiting for either a ride to crop up or a task she was qualified for. Warm days were usually slow, as folks would be more willing to walk or bike. Some days, she'd make seventy percent of the income for the week, and some days, she wouldn't make a thing.

And then there were the customers.

Her experience of folks being grateful for rides held true, as did her experience of folks having a bad day generally simply being quiet. Those types were both easy enough to deal with, if not outright enjoyable. Over time, though, she began to see a wider variety.

Around Thanksgiving, she started making trips too and from the airport and bus station, and families getting off longer trips were rarely happy. She got snapped at more than once by upset fathers trying to wrangle children or mothers coping with family through stony silence. On one occasion, played therapist along with a coyote to a frightened weasel having a panic attack, in town to visit her family and have some complicated-sounding interaction with her ex-husband.

The worst of all were the drunk folks. When she first started driving folks home from bars, it felt good. She was doing a sort of service by keeping tipsy bar-hoppers or plastered sports fans off the road. The first time someone vomited in the back seat, however, her opinion of the task began to sour. It may be nice to keep drunks from driving, but cleaning vomit out of the foot-wells — thankfully, the dog had managed to miss the seat — was hardly a pleasant task.

Football games became a source of dread. She wasn't even safe before they began, as she'd haul thoroughly pregamed fans from parties to stadium, groups of students hollering painfully loud, nigh unintelligible, whether from drink or simple in-jokey camaraderie.

The tasks from Simpletask, while a break from the enforced social interaction that was an integral part of driving, were riddled with their own problems. People generally expected that someone driving for GetThere knew what they were doing enough to leave them alone.

Not so with someone performing data entry from scanned documents or making brochures for events. She discovered a particular brand of cruelty that seemed unique to the role of small business owners, which they held in reserve for menial labor.

The lynx lost track of how many times she was called an idiot.

She lost track of the number of times she was lured in by a sizeable tip, only to have it withdrawn after she had completed the project during the three-day grace period. She lost track of how often she was brought on to be the small one, to make someone feel bigger.

Still, she had to pay the bills, didn't she?

Winter don't know how long she sat in the car, forehead resting against the steering wheel, before there was a soft knock at the driver's side window.

"Love?" Katrin's voice was muffled through the glass.

Winter looked dully out the window at the vixen, unseeing. Some part of her knew that she should get out of the car and head inside, should at the very least lift her head from the steering wheel, and yet she lacked the executive function required to even do that.

"Winter, can you come inside?"

The lynx took a deep breath. Perhaps it was the lack of something that was keeping her trapped here rather than some unwanted presence. The lack of oxygen. The lack of air. The lack of motivation.

When the breath did not bring any further energy, she let it out in a rush and, through force of will, sat up straighter and unlocked the door. She might have sat there longer, but Katrin didn't give her the chance; the door she was leaning against angled smoothly away from her.

No helping it now.

Winter unbuckled her seatbelt and accepted her wife's paw to help lever herself out of the driver's seat. Together, they shut and locked the car and made their way inside.

Only once she was settled at the kitchen table with a small plate of dill-heavy dumplings — some new recipe Katrin was testing out — was she able to loosen up.

"I'm sorry, Katrin. I just...long day."

The fox nodded, frowning. Never able to completely cease working, she seemed to be dissecting one of the dumplings she had made and was poking at the insides of it with the tip of a knife. "You've been having rather a lot of those lately, sötnos."

Winter frowned. "I suppose. I know it's not exactly ideal."

"It's okay, don't get me wrong, I'm glad to see that you're out and about doing work. I just worry."

"Yeah..."

Katrin, apparently satisfied with the internal texture of the dumpling, popped half of it in her mouth and chewed thoughtfully. When she had finished enough to do so, she continued. "Tell me about your long day, love. I want to hear, because it sounds like it was more than simply the length."

"I suppose." Winter stalled for time by eating a few of the dumplings. They were quite good, though perhaps saltier than she would have liked. "Just had a really gross ride partway through and never quite recovered."

" 'Gross' how?"

"He was just really adamant about sitting up in the front seat with me."

Some inner part of her smiled, despite the competing emotions. She knew she had Katrin's full attention when the fox finally put down her silverware. "I...see. Are you okay?" she asked.

Winter nodded. "He didn't do anything super gross physically, but it was just everything else he did."

Katrin blinked slowly, ears tilted back. Winter was never quite sure what emotion went along with such an expression, but this time, she was certain it was one of concern or worry. Perhaps anger.

"I'm alright, though, I promise. He just got really pushy about sitting up front and kept saying all these vaguely...uh, sexy things, I guess, and kept staring at me."

"Did you report him?"

"Yeah, I mentioned it on his review."

The vixen nodded.

"It just made the rest of my shift feel extra long, is all. Every time I'd go to accept a ride, I'd get nervous. I drove to the other side of town just to be sure he wouldn't request another from me."

"And did he rate you well?"

Winter winced. "No. He complained that I was unfriendly, and I got a note from the system about unacceptable behavior, like it was somehow my fault."

Katrin reached out a hand to tug one of Winter's over for a squeeze. "I'm sorry, love."

Winter returned that squeeze of the fingers distractedly. She couldn't drop the topic, though. Not now. Not after the dam had burst. "It's just so humiliating. I can't keep myself safe or I risk their ire. I can't look for jobs that pay well because I know they'll just recall the tip after and I'll be out a bunch of cash."

"It's been a month," Katrin said once the flare of anger died out. "Do you think you might look for something more traditional job again?"

"If anyone's even fucking hiring," the lynx growled.

"It's still worth looking, perhaps."

Winter bit her tongue to stay silent. It must have been evident to the fox, whose frown deepened.

"Winter, you know that I love you and won't push too hard, but this is not healthy. You have been having 'long day' after 'long day' for the last few weeks. I'm glad you can get paid for stuff like this, but I don't know if it's worth it long term, at this rate."

"You're right," she said after a long, deliberate pause. "No, you're right. I'll finish these and then start searching again."

As expected, reference to the food immediately drew the fox's attention away from the problem at hand. "Do you like them?"

"A bit salty. Maybe more lemon?"

Katrin smiled ruefully. "The salt is high, yes. I think you're just a sourpuss, though."

Winter swatted at her wife and laughed. It had been a calculated gesture, getting her to talk food, but one that she knew would distract them both. "Not as salty as you, though.

"Surprised to see you in today, Winter, and for so long."

The lynx looked up from her laptop, gratefully accepting hot chocolate number three from Malina. "I suppose I've been here for a while, yeah."

"About two hours." The badger hastened to add, "No complaints. The busier we look, the busier we get!"

The hot chocolate was good. Malina seemed to have picked up on Winter's penchant for whipped cream and piled this mug high. Something about the way the cocoa would break through the whipped cream was...not exactly soothing, and yet nonetheless she felt more at peace after.

"As long as I'm not a problem," she said.

"Not at all. Just surprised you're not driving today. Figured it'd be lunch hour rush."

Winter shrugged. "Not really feeling it lately. Had a string of creeps, so I'm mostly doing Simpletasks and looking for something more stable."

Frowning, Malina looked around The Book and The Bean and, seeing no one in need of drinks, pulled out the other chair at the lynx's table to sit. "Hopefully nothing too dramatic happened."

"No, thank goodness. Just a string of bad luck with lewd assholes." She typed at her laptop briefly, pulled up a site, and turned it toward the badger. "Apparently there's a site for reviewing drivers on a sort of hot-or-not basis, and I guess I made the list."

Malina's frown deepened. "I'd say congratulations if that weren't completely disgusting."

Winter laughed and shook her head. "Yeah, no congrats needed."

"There anything that GetThere can do about it?"

"I don't think so. They don't seem to care about the drivers all that much, truth be told. Not like I'm the first to bring it up or anything." Winter gave her hot chocolate a slow swirl, watching the skin that was starting to form on the surface ripple. "They just sent me a canned response of, like, how to stay safe as a driver."

Malina crossed her arms and leaned back in her seat. "That's frustrating. Is Simpletask treating you any better, at least?"

Something about the lynx's expression caused her to look away. They sat in silence.

"Either way." Winter tried to keep the dejection out of her voice, tried to sound positive. Tried to smile. "If you have any tips on job openings, I'm all ears."

"Well, do you know anything about coffee?"

"I...well, no. Are you hiring?"

"We've got some shifts that could use some coverage." The badger smiled, shrugged. "It's a coffee shop job. Doesn't pay much and I don't have a full-time work week's worth of shifts open, but if you're willing to learn–"

"Of course!" Winter caught herself short and laughed. "Sorry. Yeah, I'd be up to learn."

Malina's smile widened. "Great. Follow me."

Wrong-footed, the lynx tilted her head. "What, now?"

"Sure. It's fairly slow. I can at least show you around behind the bar."

She looked between the badger and her laptop, then shrugged and closed the lid, slipping it back into her bag. "Well, fuck it. Why not?"

———————————

The Book and The Bean was not enough to carry Winter, but it was enough to allow her to be more selective in her jobs. She still drove occasionally when not at the coffee shop, but the added income let her focus more on Simpletask.

What it offered beyond that was something less tangible. It leant a sense of stability that the gigs could not. She could always rely on at least a little bit of money to help supplement Katrin's income from Middagsbord. She could trust that a few shifts would help cover her share of rent, and that anything else would be covered by one-off tasks.

More than that, it eased tensions between her and Katrin.

She hadn't realized how frustrated the lack of security made her wife until she had regained it. The vixen once again became easy to talk to. She laughed more readily. She gushed about new recipes and bitched about customers. All those little things that are part of daily interactions that had been tamped down in the face of trying to make ends meet were suddenly back and in full force. That Winter was now working in food service as well certainly helped her case. They could commiserate in ways that neither had expected.

And they were happy, in their own way. A new kind of happy. A different kind. And really, what more could they ask for?

Sorting Laundry

"You always have to sort your laundry," her mother always said. "Separate the lights from the darks, at the very least. Try to get all the bright colors in one load, at least for the first few washes, than you can mix them with the dark."

Yes, ma.

"Remember how daddy got his pink shirt?"

Yes, ma.

"Just remember to sort, and you'll be fine. And don't use fabric softener on your towels, they'll stay softer that way."

Yes ma, yes ma.

She grinned, stuffing towels, light and dark together, into the machine. A bra clung to one of the towels by the hooks. She chuckled. She slid the bra up, hoping to get it off the towel without problem. She laughed. A thread tugged lose from the towel, insisting on clinging to the bra strap. She laughed harder. Laughed and laughed.

Laughter turned to sobs. Shaking sobs. Great, gasping sobs that left her clutching at the edge of the washing machine for balance. *Yes ma, yes ma. You haven't talked to me since I needed a bra, ma.* She plucked the thread from the bra and dropped both into the machine.

Your son had died, ma, and you never wanted a daughter. She admonished herself through tears about not sorting laundry.

Yes ma, sorry ma.

Morning Of

Something about the phrase 'ambulatory surgery' left the scent of opposites hanging thick in Alex's nose. It certainly wasn't actually an oxymoron, and yet here he was, sitting in the lobby, trying to pick apart why the sign felt wrong to him.

He had spent the last two days running back and forth between the couch or bed and the bathroom as the surgery prep emptied him all out. He had thought, at first, that he would be incredibly hungry on this strict fluids only diet — and then nothing but a sip of water with his meds this morning — but some combination of the laxatives and nerves made the thought of food abhorrent, and he had to force himself to stay hydrated as the magnesium citrate worked its wonders on him.

Add in the six hour drive to Portland and the complete inability to sleep during the night before, and it was no surprise that words and meaning were crowding uncomfortably inside his head.

"Alex? You ready?"

He shook himself out of his reverie. Liv was standing there, radiant as always, with an efficient-looking nurse. "Yeah."

They led him back to the pre-op room, where the young wolf stripped out of his clothes and into a hospital gown.

They shaved the back of his hand and got the IV line in place.

They gave him a pill to take 'for his nerves'.

They introduced him to the anaesthesiologist, an intense and hulking bear.

They let him shake hands with the surgeon.

And then they left him alone with Liv.

"You okay, Alex?"

He nodded, sitting on the edge of the bed. Was he? Was he anything? He didn't feel okay, but he didn't feel not-okay. "It feels what you say about flying. How you get past security, and then everything is suddenly someone else's responsibility, and all you have to do is let go and go along with what they say?"

Liv nodded.

"It's like that."

"They told me to tell you you have until they come back for you to change your mind." The older wolf's grin was sly. "I told them if you didn't keep going, I'd kick your ass."

Alex laughed. "Why's that?"

"You've been talking about this surgery non-stop for almost a year. If I had to listen to you talk about it anymore, I think I'd go nuts."

"Right." He cupped spindly hands over his breasts beneath the gown. The garment made him feel tiny, young. "I'd probably go nuts, too. It'll be so nice to be rid of 'em."

Liv's grin softened. "I know."

And then they came to take him away.

They came to whisk him down an anonymous hallway.

They came to wheel him into the OR, a room nothing like what he was expecting.

They came to ask him what music he liked.

They came to give him an oxygen mask to hold over his face.

And then he was truly in their hands.

Of Foxes and Milkshakes

Two foxes walked into a bar.

Well, okay, a diner. But most of those middle-American diners are outfitted with a bar type area, complete with red-and-chrome stools — you know the sort — which is close enough, capitalizing on that thirty-year nostalgia cycle in the way it hearkens back to the 50s or 60s. Both were full of giggles, outfitted with grins and their most casual of "nice" clothes. Somehow managing to look similar without being related, the two got along as though they were brothers. One was taller than the other, and though both were thin, he came off as lanky, whereas the shorter fox seemed more waifish — more of a track runner than his friend, the basketball player.

Although the restaurant was nearly empty — its only other customer being one of those old hound dogs who sits at the bar, perpetually nursing his second cup of coffee while staring at the gold flakes on the formica counter as if they might somehow swirl into formation to reveal the deepest secrets of the universe or maybe just the solutions to all his problems — the two convivial foxes made their way to the corner booth and plopped down across from each other.

Their animated discussion, more gossip than anything, was interrupted by a cat on roller skates popping her gum loudly by the table.

The foxes grinned up to the waitress, who, picking up on the jovial mood, beamed down at them. "What'll it be, you two?"

Straightening up, the larger of the foxes proclaimed, well rehearsed, "A vanilla shake, please, and a couple of spoons."

The waitress' eyes flicked between the two, but she said nothing, simply taking down the order before rather pointedly asking the other fox what he'd like. The smaller of the two stammered for a second, caught off guard, "Uh...c-coffee, please."

The rollercat nodded and skated on off, leaving the two foxes to glance at each other, nervous, unsure as to whether they'd committed some sort of faux pas. Each shrugged at each other at the same time and both giggled, slipping back into their animated chatter. The hum of a shake blender promised sweetness.

The feline rolled smoothly up to the table again, this time with a tray holding a shake, two mugs, and a carafe of coffee. Setting the shake pointedly before the larger fox and the two mugs in front of each of them, she poured them both a cup of coffee before zooming back to the kitchen with the kick of a skate.

The coffee sat ignored by both foxes as each grabbed a spoon from the shake, pulling it out to get that first bite: that one where the spoon's already covered with a liberal coating of shake, whipped cream, and chocolate sauce, somehow better, more complete, than the spoonfuls to follow. Coated spoons made their way into waiting muzzles and that sweetness spread like silver smiles.

With much laughter, the conversation continued, drifting from teachers, perhaps, to movies, parents, probably, to homework. Slowly, carefully, the shake was diminished, each taking care to leave the maraschino cherry standing in the middle of the glass atop a pillar of sagging whipped cream.

The talking wound down until the two were eating in silence, the taller of the foxes apparently lost in thought as he stared out the window, while the smaller watched his friend with tilted head.

"What?" asked the larger vulpine when he caught the other's gaze, muzzle painted with a lopsided grin.

Laughing, the fox shrugged and dipped his spoon in the slowly melting desert, holding it out to the taller fox. Giggling at the patently tacky yet oh-so-sweet gesture, he leaned forward to take the proffered bite. Resting his chin on his the backs of his hands, he smiled happily as he let himself be fed another few bites of the treat.

Grin softening to smile, the shorter of the two fished around in the bottom of the glass with his spoon to get at the cherry, bright red, so bright it almost glowed beneath that coating of whipped and iced cream. Picking it up delicately by the stem, he offered that as the next bite, movements slow and deliberate. The larger fox leaned forward, delicately picked the almost-too-sweet fruit from the stem, and savored. If pink had a flavor, it had to be this.

With his co-conspirator in shake-enjoyment still leaning forward, it took little enough for the smaller fox, movements deliberate — if shy — to press toward him across the table. It was fairly clear what he intended to happen next, snouts aimed at snouts, young love pinkening the insides of ears.

Clear even to the waitress, who had rolled up at this inopportune moment to refill untouched coffees. With a snap of her gum and a look hovering between disgusted and weary, she jotted something on the order pad, slapped the sheet down on the table. She grumbled, "Should'a known," and pushed off towards the kitchen.

Two foxes sat in stunned silence for several seconds as the matching blush shifted from one of embarrassment, nigh on humiliation. Shaky paws snatched at the check, the larger of the two's eyes going wide, while the smaller's welled up with tears, anti-sweet and hastily brushed away.

"Get a room queers" was written under items ordered on the check, "get out stay out" scribbled hastily at the bottom. Taking that as their cue to take their leave, the pair made a clumsy escape from the diner, followed out the door by the disdainful gaze of the roller-cat.

Once they had made it out onto the curb, warm evening air wrestling with the spreading coldness of milkshake and humiliation, the two foxes hazarded cautious glances back through the glass into the diner. The waitress watched still from behind the counter.

They decided on home instead.

They walked slowly down the street toward the larger fox's house, the closer of the two homes, in silence, very carefully not touching. The taller of the foxes kicked at the sidewalk, more trudging than walking, and the smaller fox peeked over with apologies in his eyes.

"I didn't think... I mean, I guess I shouldn't have done that..."
Nothing.

"I'm sorry, I guess I though it'd be..." he trailed off once more.

Still nothing. The larger fox was looking down at his shoes as they scuffed along the concrete, paws stuffed deep within his pockets.

"I think we should call off the rest of the night." He walked in silence for a few more steps, brow furrowed, before repeating, "We should call off the rest of the night. See you tomorrow?"

The shorter fox stood still for a stunned moment before hurrying to catch up with the taller of the two, grabbing at his elbow. "No, wait."

The taller fox stopped, but would not or could not meet his friend's gaze.

"I'm sorry," continued the smaller fox. "Please don't go."

The tall fox turned slowly and unhooked the paw from his elbow, taking it instead in his own, slipping his other free of his pocket to hold both of his friend's in his own. "I just feel weird about things, you know? If we were up in Boise, maybe, but what the heck does Sawtooth need with us?"

"Well, shucks, I do too, but..." A pause, then a defeated shrug. "It was still a nice night, wasn't it?"

A smile tickled at the corner of the taller fox's mouth and the tenseness in his posture softened. "Yeah," he said at last, nodding. "Yeah, it was still a nice night."

Shy smiles were shared, sweetness ticking back up a notch or two, then both looked down the street to where the larger fox's home lay, to the soft glow of the porch light.

The taller fox turned to look back the shorter, grunting in surprise when his muzzle clonked against another. One which had been aiming to give him a kiss on the cheek. Both blushing foxes mumbled apologies at the same time, giggled, and pressed into an awkward kiss. Noses all mushed together, lips not quite hitting their mark, and all the sweeter for it.

Two foxes stood on the sidewalk, half in light and half in darkness, working out the logistics of their first, vanilla-flavored kiss: all the little things that make fox-kissing nice, like tilting muzzles just slightly so that the nose is out of the way and standing on tip-toes, exploring new intimacies. Ears laid back and tails all aswish, still holding hands, the couple relaxed back from the kiss, bashful and giddy

Still blushing, still grinning, still paw in paw, they continued on their way to the taller fox's house.

"Times are changing," the smaller vulpine observed as they neared the low-slung suburban home. "I think for the better better."

The other fox was slow to smile, but it was an earnest one. "Yeah," he murmured, nodding slowly, as though his mind was still churning away. Sweetness still hung about them, vanilla still lingered on lips, tongues. "Y'know what? I take back what I said earlier. You want to come in for a while?"

Acknowledgements

Thanks, as always, to the polycule, who has been endlessly supportive, as well as to Sandy, Kergiby, Kayodé, Rob, Dwale (may its memory be a blessing), and many others who helped with reading and keeping me sane along the way.

Thanks also to my patrons:

$10+ Donna Karr (thanks, mom); Fuzz Wolf; green; Kit Redgrave; Merry; Orrery; Sandy; Sariya Melody

$5 Junkie Dawg; Lorxus, an actual fox on the internet

$1 Alicia Goranson; arc; Katt, sky-guided vulpine friend; Kindar; Muruski; Peter Hayes; Rax Dillon; Ruari

Madison Scott-Clary is a transgender writer, editor, and software engineer. She focuses on furry fiction and non-fiction, using that as a framework for interrogating the concept of self and exploring across genres. A graduate of the Regional Anthropomorphic Writers Workshop in 2021, hosted by Kyell Gold and Dayna Smith, she is studying creative writing at Cornell College in Mount Vernon, IA. She lives in the Pacific Northwest with her cat and two dogs, as well as her husband, who is also a dog.

www.makyo.ink